Coffee on Whiskey Road

Clint Thomas

ISBN: 979-8-8693-1218-1

ACKNOWLEDGEMENTS

A most sincere thank you to Kristen Milford for taking the time to edit this manuscript.

Thank you to my mom, Sherri Thomas, for capturing the cover photo.

And finally, thank you to the many individuals, both those that have passed and those that are still with us, who were the inspiration for the characters in this story.

Chapter 1
Good Mornings

November 3, 2011

There are a few stories about how Whiskey Road earned its name. The road happened to be one of the main avenues in the small South Carolina town of Aiken. Some local folks liked to romanticize the road's history, claiming it was the route bootleggers once used to smuggle liquor through town during Prohibition.

To honor their deeds, the town supposably once hosted annual whiskey races where people would race down the road while carrying empty bottles with them. However, nobody ever seemed to remember when such a race happened. It was quite the tall tale for a Bible Belt town where, up until recently, state law blocked the sale of alcohol on Sundays. The less exciting, albeit more accurate history was that Whiskey Road was the place where folks happened to legally transport whiskey between Atlanta and Charleston, South Carolina in the 1800s.

As Aiken grew over the decades, Whiskey Road began to look less like a rural country highway and more like a typical suburban American boulevard, becoming the primary way of getting around the southside of town. A plethora of super stores, chain restaurants, and fast-food franchises lined both sides of the now-annoyingly busy road. Whiskey Road still showed traces of Aiken's old history, particularly when driving close to downtown, but the relics of the past were now long buried under strip mall parking lots.

At six o'clock on Thursday mornings, a group of old timers always met at the Hardee's on Whiskey Road— the one next to the Home Depot. These men had been coming here for a few years now. There were five of them— ranging from ages seventy-eight to ninety. While some of these elders had been born and raised in

Aiken, a handful had moved here from elsewhere. A few still had family living in town or were married, but others were all by their lonesome. Regardless of their differences, this morning meetup had become an integral part of their weekly routine.

If they didn't have nothin' else, they knew where to get a hot cup of coffee with a few others who'd also been around the block.

Ron always managed to be the first to arrive in the morning. He was the oldest of the men. He pulled up to the fast-food joint in his '98 Chevy pickup. The truck had accumulated years of wear and tear, and the older he got, the harder it was to afford to take care of it. The way he figured, as long as the Chevy kept running, it was God's way of telling him to keep driving. That was just the kind of man he was: he was too stubborn to let good things fall apart but also too stubborn to let them change for the better.

He got out of his truck with a copy of the local newspaper in his right hand, his cane in his left. Five years ago, he finally admitted to himself that the cane was needed— but that didn't make him any less resentful. If anything, it really made him feel his age. As a young man, he had sprinted into enemy gunfire and artillery on the Pacific Islands; now, he needed assistance just to walk across a parking lot. It was hard enough being an old man, even worse being an old man who couldn't get around completely on his own.

One of the Hardee's cashiers politely greeted Ron when he walked inside. The young man, probably no older than twenty-one, recognized the senior by face but didn't know his name. Ron silently waved at the employee as he immediately walked over to the group's usual table. The quintet always sat at a booth beside the window, the one closest to the front door. While not formally reserved, everyone knew the booth was theirs. Ron sat his copy of the newspaper down on the group's table before going up to the register. The young cashier already had his coffee ready for him. Ron always took it black, double cupped, with one bag of sweetener on the side.

"Anything else for you this morning, sir?" the cashier asked, even though he already knew the answer.

Ron shook his head. "That'll be all, son."

Ron paid in cash, grabbing both the coffee and sweetener in one hand, and slowly walked back to the table. The cashier didn't offer to bring the drink to the table for Ron since he already knew that the old man would say no anyways. Besides, the heat felt soothing on Ron's stiff, arthritis-stricken fingers. Once he was seated, he began to read the front page of the newspaper. He couldn't help but groan and shake his head at most of the news. He usually saved the sports section for last, as even if there was no good news about his teams, he found it to be the most entertaining section of the paper.

After Ron finished reading the first article on the cover, he took the lid off his coffee cup to add the bag of sweetener. For most of his life, he had preferred to drink his coffee black. It wasn't until the morning of his sixty-fifth birthday when he had asked his wife, Betty, if she could toss in some sugar for him. She was surprised by the request. He half-jokingly explained to her that there were many reasons why he might become a bitter old man, but his coffee sure wasn't going to be one of them.

Betty and Ron had spent their entire lives in South Carolina. Both born and raised up in Spartanburg, they were the rare kind of high school sweethearts that never grew tired of one another. She was a year younger than him, and Ron had planned to propose to her after she graduated high school, but his plans were forcefully changed when he was called to serve in World War II. They married soon after he returned from his tour in the Pacific. When he found a steady job at a tire factory in Graniteville shortly after, the two of them planted their roots in the nearby town of Aiken.

Ten years later, the couple gave birth to their only child, a daughter named Patsy. She was named after the old country singer, Patsy Montana, an artist Ron and Betty both admired. Ron didn't see much of his daughter these days. She lived with her husband and kids all the way up in western Connecticut and didn't get much time to visit her old hometown, since she had a full-time job and teenagers to raise. At the same time, Ron was never too inclined to venture north of the Carolinas. His stubbornness had formed a rift between the two of them, one which he didn't seem too keen on fixing.

Ron was so intently focused on reading an article about how the former South Carolina governor, Mark Sanford, was going to be a political contributor to Fox News that he didn't notice Tony walk into the Hardee's.

Tony was another regular of the coffee meetup, but unlike the other men, he wasn't a Southern boy. He was the first of his Long Island, Italian American family to live in South Carolina. After retiring from running the family's wholesale seafood business, he wanted to relocate somewhere with a warm climate, welcoming people, and a slower pace—as long as that place wasn't Florida. When scouting out possible retirement locations, he, like many before him, was enamored by Aiken's quaint charm and cheaper price tag.

Despite the initial culture shock, Tony soon found himself right home in his new surroundings, and it didn't take him long to start holding doors open for everyone, drinking Carolina sweet tea in the afternoon, and learning what grits are, even if the way he talked made him stand out. Although he was no longer as boisterous as he was when he had first moved here, Ron still thought that Tony was a real character. The Long Island local's cadence reminded him of the actor, Joe Pesci— Tony even cussed like him, too.

"Ay, Ron," Tony said, grabbing his attention away from the paper.

Ron tilted the paper down and looked up. "Good mornin', Tony. How are you?"

"Oh, just fine. What's happening today?" he asked, gesturing to the newspaper.

"Well, it looks like Sanford got himself a job with Fox News."

"That old governor of yours?"

"Mhm."

Tony clicked his teeth. "Youse believe that? Guy cheats on his wife with a broad in South America, then gets a job on network television. Unbelievable. If I'd a known it was that easy to get a job in television, I woulda taken a trip down to Argentina while I was still married."

Ron shrugged. "Yeah, but we can't all go hiking on the Appalachian Trail."

"Yeah, yeah," Tony muttered. He walked over the counter to order his coffee, leaving Ron alone again to read the paper.

Ron knew that he didn't have much time to keep reading before the others arrived, so he skipped ahead to the sports section. He didn't plan to read the whole section but at least wanted to skim its cover page. At the top was the headline story about tomorrow's big local football game: Aiken High vs. South Aiken High. Pictured on the sidelines of South Aiken's practice was coach of the defensive line, Dan McMillin. The man had his arms crossed while appearing to be in the middle of yelling out orders. McMillin happened to be one of the other regulars who came to this little morning meetup.

Ron set the paper down and looked out the restaurant window when he saw Michael pull up to the parking lot. The only non-white guy of the group, Michael had the oldest working vehicle of all the guys, an '87 Ford Ranger GT. It was thanks to his expert handiwork that the pickup truck was still running. Ever since he was a kid growing up in the historically Black neighborhood of Sol Legare Island outside of Charleston, Michael had always been interested in cars. He learned about their inner workings when he served in the Korean war, after which a serviceman got him a job at a repair shop in Augusta. He worked there for close to ten years until he finally acquired the knowledge and credibility to open his own tires and brakes shop in Aiken. These days, he was still the shop owner on paper, but his nephew was the one running the garage.

Michael slowly made his way towards the Hardee's. The old man walked with a slight slouch, due to an outstanding injury to his lumbar that had made him retire earlier than he would have liked. As he walked through the doors, he greeted Ron with a salute. Ron returned the gesture. This tradition was something that only they did with each other, since they were the only veterans in the group. Michael ordered his coffee with a half and half, and he took a seat on the opposite side of the booth from Ron, next to Tony. Michael softly groaned as he sat down— even sitting down wasn't as easy as it used to be.

"Well, good mornin', fellas," Michael greeted both.

"Good morning."

"How are y'all?" asked Michael.

Tony answered, "Besides my damn neck being stiff— feels like I'm walking around wit' a brick on it— can't complain."

Always a man of few words, Ron simply replied, "I'm just peachy." He flipped the paper around to show them the picture on the cover. "Look who made the paper this morning."

Tony and Michael both squinted to see.

Tony mumbled, "Didn't bring my readers."

Michael was the first to notice Coach McMillin standing in the background. "Well, I'll be," he said with a hearty chuckle.

Tony finally realized what Ron was trying to show him. "Ah, why the hell did they put that guy on the cover for? Gonna scare away readers."

Ron and Michael both laughed at his comment.

Ron asked, "Y'all goin' to the big game tomorrow?"

Michael and Tony shook their heads.

"After we get done here, I'm actually headin' on down to Charleston the whole weekend for some family business," Michael explained.

Concerned, Ron was about to ask for details, but Tony chimed in first, bragging, "And I made other plans, too. Got dinner with a lady tomorrow night."

Michael and Ron both raised their eyebrows with curiosity.

Intrigued, Michael asked, "Ohh, a new lady friend. Who might the gal be?"

"A neighbor of mine. She lives a few doors down from me. Moved here a few weeks ago from Virginia to help take care of her older sister or something, I don't remember. Anyways, important things that she's a bit younger than me, and a whole lot better looking," Tony explained with a devilish grin.

"You old hound dog," said Michael as he took his first sip of coffee.

Ron asked, "Where you fixin' to take her?"

"The Wilcox," Tony said, with a wink.

The other two men were amazed. The restaurant of the Wilcox Hotel was one of the fancier joints in town, definitely the kind of place to take someone if you were looking to make a good first impression.

Michael hooted, "Lordy, she sure must be somethin' special."

Tony was getting a little annoyed. "Alright, alright, easy, easy. Let's not get too far ahead of ourselves here, huh? Jeez, both of youse should go on a date."

"Ah, no need to put a woman through that," replied Michael, laughing at his own self-effacing joke.

Tony then turned to Ron. "And what's your excuse, huh?"

Ron explained, "Sheww, I'm too old to be datin' anyone."

Tony took this opportunity to bust Ron's balls a little. "Too old? You? Please! Don't you want to get around some more? I mean, when was the last time you even took a lady out on a date, huh?"

Before taking another sip of his coffee, Ron shrugged. "I suppose I couldn't tell you." It was a simple answer to calmly shut down the subject, but also an honest one.

It had been well over a decade since he tried dating anyone. Ron had been in his sixties when his wife passed away. They were lucky to have had a picturesque marriage. Of course there had been ups and downs, smooth sailing and rough patches, but they always stuck happily together. Betty's absence had been, and continued to be, a tough adjustment to make. The few women he dated afterwards, to no fault of their own, were unable to connect with him. He simply wouldn't let them. He had to ask himself how Betty put up with him for all those years. "Perhaps I was just high maintenance," Ron would tell himself. But the real reason, the one he would never admit to himself: At the ripe old age of ninety, what point was there?

Ron stopped pondering to himself when he heard the men greet Coach McMillin. The elderly football player limped into the Hardee's, walking with a cane due to a hip replacement and years of being noticeably overweight. Back in his heyday, he played on the defensive line for The Georgia Bulldogs. With the way that his cheeks drooped, he sort of looked like a bulldog, too. After his college career ended, he returned to his hometown of Aiken where he became a coach and history teacher at South Aiken High. He had a reputation for being a strict teacher and a disciplined coach, but people knew him as a jolly and loving man outside of work. Although he officially retired from the education system a decade ago, he still coached the linemen as a volunteer.

No one except for his wife called him by his first name, Dan. Everyone around town referred to him as Coach. His profession had melded with his identity, and he was perfectly fine with that. Although he was the youngest man of the group— only still in his seventies— he often spoke as though he was the wisest of all of them, even if he wasn't the smartest.

"Good mornin' there, men," he acknowledged the group, making his way to the register.

He was the only one that took his coffee decaf. Diabetes was to thank for that. Once he had his drink in hand, he took his seat in the booth next to Ron.

Ron moved the paper over to Coach, pointed at the picture, and said, "Look who they put on the cover this morning."

Coach quickly saw himself in the picture. He shook his head with a chuckle. "O'lordy, they just had to go and embarrass me like that."

Tony asked, "How's the team lookin' for tomorrow, Coach?"

"Why don't you go ahead and tell us the game plan," demanded Michael.

Coach sighed. "Men, we can talk about the game in a little bit, but I got some bad news I need to share with y'all first."

He paused to clear his throat. The other men sat up straight, leaning in a little closer, expressing concern about what Coach was going to say.

In a calm but somber tone, Coach continued. "Jill got a call last night from Maggie. Y'all… there's no easy way to say this, but Rick had a stroke yesterday mornin'. He didn't make it."

Chapter 2
Funerals

Rick was by no means a saint, no one truly was, but he had been a good man. If there was one quality that people would remember about him, it would be his kindness towards his neighbors.

His life was simple, blessed, and humble. Aside from his time as a student at the University of South Carolina in Columbia, he had spent his whole life in Aiken. He met his wife, Maggie, while pursuing his degree in business. After graduation, they married and settled back down in his hometown where he made a living as a successful realtor.

Both Maggie and Rick were the type of people that seemed to know everybody in Aiken. They actively volunteered in charities, church endeavors, and their kids' extracurriculars. Whenever they ran errands or went out to eat, they would always get stuck talking to people who knew them from somewhere or another. Obviously, there were times when that got annoying, but they always responded with sincere smiles and warm conversation. Maggie and Rick may have lived modestly, but their lives were rich with people that cared about them.

Rich with people that would surely mourn Rick's passing.

The men sitting around the table were visibly shaken by the news. Out of all of them, Rick was the person they least expected to pass away without warning. He had always been so full of life; it was hard for them to accept that he was actually gone. After Coach shared the news, all they could do was sit in silence— partially out of respect, partially from shock. The only sounds were coughs, grunts and sighs.

After some time, Michael finally broke the silence. He calmly asked Coach, "How's Maggie holding up?"

Coach shook his head. "Bout how you'd expect— not good. Jill's goin' over there later this mornin' so she don't gotta be by her lonesome. The kids will get into town later this afternoon. Sounds like, you know, they really wanna be here for their mama."

Tony chimed in, "Is there a funeral scheduled yet, or is it too soon to know?"

Coach shrugged. "Jill said that Maggie was hopin' to have it by Sunday. Um, I'm sure the kids'll get the arrangements in stone later on today or tomorrow. I'll let y'all know when and where it'll be."

They all quietly nodded their heads. No one teared up or so much as frowned but instead simply furrowed their brows, kept their mouths sternly flat, and stared blankly at their individual cups of coffee. This was the way that many old Southern men processed bad news.

An onlooker might have thought this method of mourning unconventional, but the men were at an age where the relationship with death was a bit more complicated. Attending funerals for siblings, cousins, friends, neighbors— all had become a common occurrence. The pool of people they had known forever was drying up. At each of these funerals, a thought always lurked at the back of their minds: count their blessings because Lord knows when it could be their turn to rest in the open casket.

Ron finally broke the extended silence. "He was a good man. Sheww, a good friend, too."

The other men muttered in agreement, trailing off. "Oh, yeah, yeah. Yes, sir…"

"If memory serves me right, he's the one who put this whole mornin' thing together," Michael pointed out, making a circular motion with his hand while pointing at the table.

"That's right, that's right," agreed Coach. "Definitely a good man. Always been a hard worker, too."

"Mhm, mhm," they murmured collectively.

Tony told them, "I bet wherever that funeral is, it's gonna be a full house."

"Mhm, mhm."

"I figure it'd be at his church," said Ron. "Maggie and him are both— well, they were heavily involved with volunteering and outreach there."

"Couldn't go anywhere with him without folks striking up a conversation who knew him," Michael told them, shaking his head at the memory with a faint smile on his face.

"That guy was Mr. Popular," said Tony as he began to reminisce out loud. "Yeah, back when I moved down here, you know, he was one of the first people I met. I was trying out one of the public golf courses in town on my own. He was in a group of three in front of me, playing slow as hell. You guys remember that he couldn't play golf for shit."

The men all laughed at the anecdote. They had all either played a round with Rick, or at least had heard about his terrible luck on the golf course. Everyone would always let him take a few extra mulligans.

Tony continued. "Anyways, instead of just letting me play on through like you would expect, he invites me to join their group. So, we get to talking— nearly talked my damn ear off 'cause I wasn't used to that yet, you know what I'm saying? A couple hours later, I'm having lunch with the guy, forgetting that I just met him. He treated me like we'd been pals for years. Thanks to Rick, I ended up meeting a lot of people around town. He showed me the best places to eat— to drink. The son of a bitch wasn't even Catholic but somehow knows the names of the different bishops in the region. He was un-freakin-believable. How the hell did he have time not just to meet everyone, but remember them? How do you do that?"

Coach shifted himself around in the booth to sit up straight. He often had to adjust because of his hip. "That's just the kinda man he was. It kept him busy, that's for sure," he said, groaning.

After taking a sip of coffee, Michael spoke. "You know, I can't say I remember when exactly I first met him, but I know that he was one of my regulars at the shop. He always came in to get the tires on his Chevies fixed. He always drove Chevies. When my nephew started takin' on more responsibility in the garage, and I was finding myself behind the desk more, Rick and I would eventually get to talkin' to pass the time. Can't lie, there were times when he'd get to annoyin' you. I tell you what, he'd talk your ear off if you'd let him." Michael paused to chuckle at the memory.

He continued. "After a while, he finally invited me to do something outside of work. Oh, gosh, I think it was to either watch a game or have dinner with 'em, back before Tina and I separated— memory's gettin' too fuzzy these days. Whatever the case, we became friends after that."

The men did the thing again where they all silently nodded along. They were too prideful to show their grief, taught from upbringing that this tactic was how "real" men should act around company.

Ron thought he should also say something about Rick. He could talk about how he met Rick because both of their daughters were on the same young softball team that Ron volunteered to coach. There was the weekend-long fishing trip the two of them took down in the marshes of the ACE Basin near Beaufort. Maybe he could tell the men how much it meant to him that Rick was more than willing to be a pallbearer at Betty's funeral. There were years of history he could recite.

However, being the quiet and reserved man that he was, Ron didn't say anything. He didn't feel comfortable sharing— not because he was embarrassed, but these were memories that he would rather keep to himself. He had grown far too accustomed to keeping things to himself, a problem that was only getting worse as the years went on. Perhaps in time he would share the stories so they didn't disappear with him, but for now, he only knew how to let sleeping dogs lie.

Coach cleared his throat. "Back in high school, and I'm doin' my best to remember that far back now, I think Rick would've been two years ahead of me. I remember meetin' him when we were both on the varsity football team. Now, I'm not tryin' to bad mouth the man or anything, but I'll tell y'all what, he was only on it because he was a senior."

The other men couldn't help but laugh at the observation.

With a smile, Coach clarified. "Hey now, hey now, I said I'm not tryin' to bad mouth. If he was here, I guarantee y'all he'd say the same thing. Anyways, um, I remember doing drills and playing against him at practice. His play wasn't nothin' to write home about, but I tell y'all what now, that man was one of the most dedicated players on the team that year. I'll give him that. His biggest strength was his heart. Just watchin' the way he carried himself, the man had heart."

The men nodded their heads, murmuring sentiments like "yes, sir" and "he sure did."

Coach continued with his story that was quickly turning into an impromptu eulogy. "And you know, that's how he lived. That's how he lived his whole life. He had a big heart for all the folks around him. Nowadays, you don't get too many men who'll treat people that good for no reason. He was a rare breed, and that's why folks are gonna remember him many years from now. They're gonna remember that big ol' heart of his, the one that he was *always* happy to share." He emphasized the last point by knocking on the table with his fist.

Once more, the men were silent as they reflected on the life of their friend. A life filled with dedication, loyalty, discipline, respect, and gratitude. A good life that still had more to give and that deserved to leave this world under more peaceful circumstances. Although they didn't say anything, all the men could agree that his sudden passing was nothing but a damn shame.

Their reflective moment of silence went on for about another minute until Tony lifted up his cup of coffee. "Hey, to Rick."

The other men chuckled at Tony trying to toast with a paper cup of coffee but also joined in on the gesture.

"To Rick!"

They gently clinked the paper cups together, doing their best not to spill any coffee on the table.

After their toast, Ron took it upon himself to make things more lighthearted. He told them, "Y'all know what? I know if Rick was still here, he'd be at that ball game tomorrow hollerin' for South Aiken to get a win."

The other men heartily agreed. "Yeah, yeah, mhm…"

With a laugh, Michael said, "He'd cheer so loud that I remember folks askin' him which player was his kid or grandbaby. They were always surprised when he'd explain that his kids and grandbabies already graduated, he was just a passionate alum."

The men continued to laugh as they reminisced on the memories of Rick being rambunctious, pleasantly so, at the high school games. Even if South Aiken was losing miserably, he always got the fans in the non-student sections to come alive. He had a way of igniting that spark in others.

Finally steering towards a new topic, Tony asked Coach, "Alright, Coach, so how's the team looking for tomorrow?"

Chapter 3
Sports

Of the two high schools in town, South Aiken was generally considered the better one for academics, which wasn't saying much. The South Aiken Thoroughbreds also had a hell of a men's soccer team and a lady's golf team. Both had won state a couple years back, but the same could not be said for the football program.

The football team typically only won four games a season— four out of twelve games. The Thoroughbreds' claim to fame was being featured in a blurb in *Sports Illustrated*. The honor? Being the team estimated to have the worst losing streak to a crosstown rival of any high school football team in America. Needless to say, people were hopeful for an upset at tomorrow night's game, but nobody in their right mind would bet on it.

Sitting around the table with the men, Coach explained. "Y'all been to some of our home games this season. Y'all seen the boys. Some of these young men, if they really stick with it now, I can see playing college ball. No doubt about it. The other ones now…" Coach stopped to shake his head in frustration, crossing his arms. "Some of them just can't focus up! I really do think that all the young men on the team have their heart in it. I believe that, or at least I like to think so. But when push comes to shove, when they're in the heat of the moment, they keep on losin' sight of the goal. Y'all following me?"

Without answering Coach's question, Tony asked, "So you think tomorrow is gonna be a bust?"

Coach shook his head while laughing. "Hey now, I didn't say no such thing. Look, it's gonna be tough, but the team has been real wile up all week. They want this win!"

"I wish y'all could have another player like y'all did a few years back with Domnic Hamilton," said Michael. The men all nodded their heads in agreement. They all remembered the name.

"I tell y'all what, that kid was a fine runnin' quarterback," Ron added.

Coach reminisced with a grin. "O'lordy, Hamilton was somethin' else. Wasn't just a good quarterback, but he could also be runnin' back, receiver, tight end, safety. At practice, if we needed a position filled, it didn't matter what it was, he was always ready to jump in. Definitely a talented ball player who worked his tail off."

"I haven't talked to his mama or daddy in a while, but he ended up at Coastal, right?" Michael asked.

Coach nodded. "Yes, sir! That's right. He really wanted to go to Clemson. That's what he used to always tell everyone. When push came to shove, Clemson said they might take him with no guarantee that he might ever play, but Coastal was the only one who offered him a full ride. I don't think he aspired to go pro, just wanted to play college ball, so he took it as an opportunity to get a degree. And really, I can't say I blame him. He's out there buildin' a future for himself. That's a responsible young man right there. Anyways, I hear he's doin' good on the team. They got him as one of their startin' runnin' backs."

Coach had a tendency to go off on tangents, especially when talking about football. His friends were all too familiar with the habit.

In an effort to get Coach back on course, Tony chimed in. "No doubt about it, we all like a star player, but they don't win games alone. There's something I really want to know: what does the head coach think about tomorrow, eh? I mean— and I'm not trying to be too disrespectful or anything— but his record isn't looking the best the last few seasons, to say the least."

Coach frowned for a brief moment. "Now Coach West, despite what folks been sayin', is a good coach. Good man, too. I'm not ignorant about how students and parents feel about him. And you know, he's said it himself: he ain't dumb, but he ain't smart neither." Despite the serious tone, Coach couldn't help but chortle at that remark. "Fellas, the point I'm tryin' to make here is that Coach West, although he ain't gettin' through to every player on the team, he's still a heck of a football coach. He's just like me in that he's been around the game his whole life. He knows what it takes to make a team win."

Tony wasn't satisfied with the response. "Well, that's an answer the local paper might like, but if I was Coach West, I'd be concerned about my job at this rate. Don't get me wrong, this is still high school ball we're talking about, but there comes a point where the principal won't be okay with all these losing seasons, you know what I'm saying?"

At that moment, Coach lost his patience. He lowered his voice to make a vague, simple warning. "Tony, I wouldn't much concern yourself with none of that. Ya clear?"

Tony raised his hands up a tad to signal a truce. "Sure thing," he mumbled.

Coach shook his head as the atmosphere around the table grew tense.

In an effort to make the conversation light-hearted again, Michael jokingly asked, "Coach, how many more seasons is Jill gonna let you work until she makes you retire a second time?"

Coach let out a laugh. "I tell y'all what, if any of y'all asked me that back when I first retired, I'd say only one or two more seasons at most. Now she's gone and started likin' havin' me away at night. She likes getting the house to herself. Lordy, If I told her, 'Honey, I think this will be my last season coaching,' she'd probably say, 'The hell it ain't!'"

The group of guys all laughed together, most noticeably Tony who was still trying to get back on Coach's good side. They all knew that although Coach and his wife loved one another dearly, the man easily got on her nerves. After being married for over fifty years, she was bound to be annoyed by him.

After the laughter subsided, Coach continued. "But you know, she understands. She knows that after being stuck with me for so many years, football is just a part of me. It's why even though I say I'm retired, I still get up to go out there, and teach the next generation of young men. I know it ain't much, but it's a small service I can do. Keeps me from getting too old, too quickly. Suppose I'll keep on at it till the other coaches tell me to get lost."

"You just love the game, don't ya?" Michael posed, more as a statement of fact rather than an actual question.

Coach nodded with a big grin. "Yes, sir! Yes, sir. Ever since I was youngin', it's been a part of me." He took a sip of his coffee. "Y'all ever felt that way about the sports you played?"

Michael shook his head. With a click of his teeth, he explained, "I still got some memories of playin' different ball games with my sisters and other kids down the street. Never did play any sports in school. Y'all need to remember now, growin' up back then was a lot different for me than y'all. Me, my sister, and all the other kids in the neighborhood did our schoolin' in the Farmers Lodge building. There were activities and games we would play after school but nothin' like league sports. Let me tell ya, Coach, what football was for you, was what fishin' with my daddy was for me."

"He was a big fisherman?" Coach asked.

Michael nodded his head. "He was always fishin'. If we didn't know where he was, a good guess was that he was down at the water. I still got some fond memories of headin' out to the marsh with him at the crack of dawn. He taught me a lot down there on the banks, both about fishin' and bein' a man. We didn't just fish but also caught crabs, some oysters. It felt good comin' back with the day's catch. Nowadays, when I'm able to get out to fish, it don't matter if it's in the upstate, Lake Murray, or back in the Lowcountry, it always takes me back. It takes me back to those to those simpler times…"

Michael trailed off. His mind was off visiting a different place from long ago— a place that only he remembered, even if the memory was a bit fuzzy.

Coming back to the present, he continued. "Sorry, must've trailed off there." He turned to Tony sitting next to him. "Tony, you mentioned before you come from a big baseball family."

"Oh, yeah. As far back as I can remember, we were hooked on it."

"Y'all are Yankees fans, right?" Coach jokingly asked.

Tony rolled his eyes. "Alright, wise guy, I know you know that we're all Mets fans!"

The other men laughed. They were always amused by how easy it was to give the northerner a hard time.

Tony continued. "As I was saying, I played ball in my younger days. My brothers did, too. I only played up through high school. I enjoyed it, but I don't got the same, uh, fondness about it like you two do with your things," he said, motioning towards Coach and Michael.

Just when Tony appeared to be done speaking, a thought popped into his head. "Actually, I was just remembering, when I was a kid, and I mean *really* little, we'd all go to Mets games, around four to five times a season. Tickets were cheaper back then. Me, my big brothers, my ma and pop, we'd all go. Those were some good times, maybe even the best. When I was around eight or nine, that's when my parents split up. Like I told you guys before, Ma found out he was sleeping around and all that. I'm not gonna bring all that up again, but what I'm getting at is that my memories of going to those games— I guess you could say as one big happy family— well, those are special times that I sometimes think about.

"But anyways, enough of this sentimental crap." Tony quickly pivoted. "Point is I've always liked baseball, and I've always liked The Mets. End of story."

After snickering a little bit at how Tony ended his story, Coach said, "Don't worry about it, Tony. If Rick was here, he'd say a lot of the same. He was always involved with his daughters' sports. I know one did softball, and I think the other did…What was it?"

Ron chimed in with the answer. "If I recall, it was volleyball."

Coach snapped his fingers with the realization. "Ah, yeah, that's right. The youngest played volleyball up through college. Anyways, one thing that Rick always told me was somethin' like, 'The best thing about sports isn't always the game, but the camaraderie between players, and the camaraderie between the fans.'"

Michael laughed. "Yeah, he also said somethin' like that to me, one time or another."

"I tell y'all, he loved tryin' to sound all philosophical, am I right?" Coach laughed. "But you know, the man had a point. I've never exactly put it that way, both because some of the boys don't understand, and I'm not the best with comin' up with big words on the spot—"

The other men laughed at the remark.

Coach continued. "Hey now, hey now, stay with me here, alright. But y'all see? That's sort of the lesson I try to drill into the heads of these young men. If you're willin' to work hard together, y'all gonna get better both on and off the field."

Michael recited, "As iron sharpens iron, so one person sharpens another."

"Which book is that from? Proverbs?" Coach asked.

Michael nodded. "Proverbs."

"That's what I thought. Glad I can still remember some things," said Coach. "Anyways, I promise I'll stop running my trap about this in a second. What I'm gettin' at is that Rick really found a way to grow bonds between his family through sports. You want to talk about a real volleyball or softball dad, he's a textbook case."

The men around the booth nodded in agreement. "Yes, sir, sure was," they said in some form or another, taking a break from conversing to drink more of their coffees. It was less about the fact of finishing their drinks before the cups got cold and more about the men enjoying a moment of quiet— they didn't need to constantly be talking in order to have a good morning. All that was needed was good company.

Ron took this quiet time to look out the window to his left. He wasn't staring at anything in particular but was more so absorbed in his own thoughts. The talk of sports and family brought back memories of when he coached Patsy's ten-year-old softball team.

Coaching softball had been a fun pastime for Ron's little family. He could still remember how his daughter would smile at him when she would make it to a base, how Betty would cheer them on from the bleachers, and how proud he was of the girls for always playing their hearts out. Those were some golden days, a time when Betty was still around, and before there was any animosity between him and Patsy— days that were long gone. Even the memories were starting to fade.

He finally realized one of the men at the table was saying his name. "...Hello, Ron! Ron!"

Ron was startled out of his daydream. "Oh, I apologize. Suppose I was staring a little too much off into space."

"You feeling alright there, Ronnie?" Tony asked.

The question made Ron roll his eyes— he hated being called Ronnie. "Yeah, Tony, I'm peachy. Guess I got caught reminiscin' too much."

Tony nodded. "Ah, that's good you're thinking back, 'cause I was trying to ask if you played baseball back in high school. I mean, that was your sport and all, right?"

"It was the game I enjoyed the most, you're right about that. But believe it or not, I didn't play on my high school team."

"No?" asked Tony.

Ron shook his head. "Nope. I played Little League for Lord knows how many years when I was a youngin'. Sheww, probably played in a game nearly every weekend of my boyhood. By the time I got started high school, I wasn't all that particular on keepin' it up."

Coach raised an eyebrow. "Well now, from what I understand, or at least from what I've been told, you were a fine shortstop in Little League. What on earth changed your mind?"

Without thinking about it, Ron told him, "I was more concerned with music in those days."

As soon as the words came out of his mouth, Ron winced, surprised that he had let that slip. He used to be more open about the hobby in his younger days. Once Patsy was born, though, he never spoke about it outside of his family. Music was something that he was intensely private about, not due to embarrassment but more so he regretted giving up on the passion when he did. He didn't like dwelling on what could've been.

The other men around the table were surprised. In all these years, they never knew he had an interest in music, so it was an unexpected tidbit of news. The men all assumed that Ron lived, for lack of a better way of putting it, a fairly square life. Not that he was boring to be around, but they never figured him for going too far off the straight and narrow, so their interest was piqued.

Coach was the first to say anything. "Oh, really? I don't remember you ever sayin' anything about that. Were you in the school band or somethin'?"

Ron sighed and clicked his teeth. "No, no. Never was with the marchin' band or such."

"Then what was it then?" Tony asked bluntly.

"I'm curious about this, too," echoed Michael.

Ron let out a seasoned groan. "If y'all have to know…" He hesitated for a second before elaborating further, observing the eager looks on their faces. "I was really into playin' folk and bluegrass."

"Wow!" The men all exclaimed in different ways, finally finding out something new about a man they had known for years. They started barraging Ron with a volley of comments and questions:

"Wow, I would've never figured."

"You play the banjo?"

"Were you in a band or something?"

"Sounds like you could've been the original Tennessee Ford."

"Can you sing?"

"You should think about playin' somethin' for us."

Although they meant well, the men were rapidly getting under Ron's skin. He never meant to share this piece of trivia with them which might seem like a silly thing to be so secretive about, but that was just how he felt: exposed.

He put a palm up as a signal for them to stop. "Okay, alright, alright. Y'all look here now. This is somethin' I prefer to keep to myself. Wish I hadn't said anything. I'm at that age where I sometimes speak before thinkin'. So look, back in school, I picked up the guitar, and started playin' the songs I heard comin' down from the Blue Ridge and Charlotte. Played here and there for some friends, some parties. That's about the thick of it, and if y'all would be so inclined, that's all I'm gonna say about that."

The other men, however, were not ready to move on from the topic.

Michael asked, "Wait just a minute there. Did Betty know about it?"

Ron sighed. "She did, she did." Even though he wanted to stop talking about it, he couldn't help but smile as the memory of their first meeting came back to him. "It's actually how I caught her eye," he confessed to the men.

Tony smirked. "Damn, no kidding? Seem to remember you telling me the two of youse met at a tailgate or something."

"That's right. She heard me playin' some Gene Autry. I wanna say the song was "Left My Gal In The Mountains." We struck up a conversation, and the rest is history."

Coach gave Ron a pat on the back. "You sly dog. She must've liked what she heard. I knew that you and her were always big country fans. Now I think I know why."

Still prying, Tony asked, "You still play at all?"

"Oh, no, no." Ron answered swiftly. "Haven't touched the guitar in Lord knows how long, and I don't particularly care to."

"You know, you could always pick it back up," Michael gently suggested.

Ron let out another audible groan, clearly ready to shift the topic of discussion off of him. "No, no, my fingers don't move like they used to. Even if they did, I doubt I would remember a single note. Anyways, that was a long time ago. I'm thankful for having it as a pastime in school. It kept me busy. Didn't give me time to start drinkin' or doin' dope, like some boys these days. Coach, who's that one player you mentioned before who had that problem?"

Ron already knew the answer to the question but he wanted Coach to go on a tangent— the perfect way to get their attention off of Ron's past.

"Oh, Lordy," Coach began, taking a deep breath. "Trevor Dunn. Now that's a young man who had it made!"

Michael and Tony both rolled their eyes, each having heard this story one too many times.

Coach continued. "He had the makin's of a great football player. He could play soccer real good, too. And Lord Almighty, he was fast. He ran somethin' like a four point seven— four point eight, forty. In my whole career, I'd never seen— and I'm sorry to bring race into it— but I'd never seen a white kid be that agile for his height. Then off the field, he got to grow up in a nice big house over in Woodside with the sweetest mama and daddy. Both of them were so successful. If he didn't get a sports scholarship, his folks had the money to send him to any school in the country.

"Then come junior year, somethin' changed. He started messin' around with some boys who thought they were hot shit. Started gettin' into trouble with smokin', partyin', fightin'. I still remember overhearin' some Monday mornin' gossip about how he'd gotten booked over the weekend for smokin' grass in a McDonald's parkin' lot. How the hell do you have it made like that, and you just go and throw it all away?" Coach shook his head, letting out a heavy sigh. "I know we all did our own stupid things growin' up, but Trevor Dunn is a perfect example of what happens young men get too blinded by the wilds of youth and stop lookin' ahead. Y'all know what I mean?"

Chapter 4
Vices

In response to Coach's story, Tony said, "Yeah, yeah. But you know something? We all did a little fooling around back in our time. When it comes to being wild, young and reckless, shit, I'm guilty as charged. And you schmucks don't act like you're innocent of that, okay? What I will say, and it's sort of going off what you're saying about that Dunn kid, Coach, is that the kids these days are something else! The sort of shit they get into, versus what the little bit of trouble we used to get into, it's unbelievable!"

"Lordy, that's for sure," said Michael. He straightened up in his seat as he continued. "And look here, I'm by no means without sin, but I didn't *ever* act as reckless as young folks do these days. We got boys out here gettin' into fights for no reason, other than just to brag that they've been in a fight. Hell, even girls are, too!"

Coach nodded along. "That's for sure. When the boys on the team don't think I'm listenin', I've heard them talk about all sorts of debauchery them other kids get into! I tell y'all, back when we were growin' up, we'd just get into trouble while havin' fun. Now kids are gettin' into trouble simply for the sake of makin' trouble."

"And look, to their credit, they're having to grow up through two wars, a recession, and the Obama administration," Tony added with a twinge of sympathy. "I'm sure none of those things are comforting. At the same time, though, that's no excuse for their behavior."

Ron hadn't intended to get the men all riled up; he only wanted them to turn their attention away from him. He put his palm on his forehead in frustration. Was asking for a relaxing morning too much?

"I tell y'all," Coach started in, "I couldn't even tell y'all how many young men I've had to sit down to discuss their misbehavin'. And look, I apologize for gettin' so heated about this, but it really worries me how this generation handles conflict. They can't let things go. I don't know if I can completely agree with you, Michael, that they're gettin' into fights for no reason, but their reasons sure ain't good ones. It's childish. They don't know how to let things go nowadays. It's why I've never been in a fight."

Tony rolled his eyes in disbelief. "Oh, come on! You're telling me, telling *all* of us, that you've never been in a fight before?"

Coach feverishly shook his head. "Never."

Tony wasn't convinced. "Look at you. You're a big lineman. I know hotheads would've been lining up to make a name for themselves by taking a swing at you. I remember how boys at my high school were. And just so we're all clear, I know for a fact this isn't just some New York thing."

"Tony, I'm tellin' ya, I ain't never been in no fight. I saved it for the field. I never had no business fighting no—" Coach paused for a moment. He seemed to finally remember something. With a shrug, he told them, "Alright, well I suppose I'd be lyin' if I said that. Tell y'all what though, I ain't never lost a fight."

The men around the table laughed at the confession. Coach chuckled right along with them, too.

As the laughter died down, Tony cleared his throat, speaking in a hushed voice. "You know, I recently found out that my third oldest grandson, I think he's a sophomore in high school now or something, he got caught sneaking out and joyriding a month ago."

"No kiddin'?" asked Coach.

"Yeah, can you believe it? I always thought that out of all the grandkids, he was the most well-behaved one. Always doing well in school, staying out of trouble, yada yada. Couldn't believe it when his dad, my oldest son, called a couple weeks ago to tell me about the pile of shit he'd gotten in. So, a few months ago, I think it was August, he snuck out in the middle of the night, pushed his dad's car down the driveway, and drove off to meet with his friends! For crying out loud, he's only fifteen! He doesn't even have a license yet."

"What good reason did he have for meetin' up with his friends all that late?" Michael asked, curious.

The more Tony spoke on the topic, the angrier he got. "Supposedly, he was only meeting them at a twenty-four-hour diner. That's what he claims. Even if that's true, he risked his whole future over a midnight stack with his buddies. What would've happened if he'd gotten pulled over, you know what I'm saying? How the hell are you gonna do something that damn stupid? And let me tell you guys, I've been to that diner before, so take my word for it, the food's not worth it."

The men laughed at that last bit, to Tony's annoyance.

Michael could sense Tony's palpable frustration. "I apologize for that, Tony." He cleared his throat before continuing. "So how did your grandson get caught?"

Tony grinned— not a joyful grin but a grin rooted from a place of holding back anger. "Oh, you schmucks are gonna love this part. So get this, it's the middle of the night, his dad is fast asleep. Suddenly, bang! He wakes up to the sound of metal crashing and brakes screeching. He runs outside to see what's what. So, what happened is that while pulling into the driveway, my grandson turned too hard, ended up running over the goddamn mailbox!"

Coach shook his head while trying his best not to laugh. "Oh, Lordy. Well, Tony, all I can say is that I hope your grandson learned his lesson. I know we're all chucklin', and I apologize for that, but we'd be madder than a hornet if one of our grandkids did that, too. Thankfully, they haven't."

Michael added, "Mhm, it's like you said, Coach, kids these days are gettin' into trouble just for the sake of gettin' into trouble.

I don't know about y'all, but even as a kid who grew up obsessed with cars, that's somethin' I would've never done."

All the men nodded their heads in agreement— except for Ron. He was sitting on a story that he had never told them, only this one he didn't mind sharing.

"You know what y'all? I can't believe I'm admittin' this, but I've…" Ron couldn't help but giggle a little before finishing his sentence. "Yeah, I've done a little somethin' like that before."

The other men stopped and stared at Ron in shock.

"You?" Tony exclaimed.

"Alright, you gotta tell us this one," Coach said.

"I figure I must've been sixteen or seventeen. I didn't have a license or nothin', but my daddy had taught me how to drive his truck. At that time, I'd been flirting with this young lady named Martha Lou." Ron's cheeks blushed at the mere mention of the name.

"Was she dropped dead gorgeous?" Tony asked, unsurprisingly.

"Y'all have no idea. She even got elected homecomin' queen later on in our senior year. Couldn't believe that out of all the boys at the school, she was interested in me. Now, she was a lot more popular than I was, so I knew that if I was gonna impress her, I was really gonna have to knock her socks off. She suggested that we go to this spot along the Pacolet River. It had the reputation of bein' a Lover's Lane at the time. I told her how I'd love to drive her there in 'my truck.' Obviously, I didn't have a truck, and my daddy wasn't gonna let me use his to impress a girl. So, I snuck out around 11:30 at night when he was already asleep, picked her up, we had an okay time—"

"Just an okay time?" Tony raised his eyebrows. "That's it?"

Ron laughed. "Don't get your hopes up. Nothin' too excitin' happened. We just didn't hit things off. So come later, I'm almost back home after dropping her off, thinkin' I'm about to get off scot-free. Now just to set the scene for y'all, our garage was separate from the house. It was a cheap little thing made of flimsy metal, practically a free-standing awning. I should've just put the truck in neutral to push it in. Instead, I thought I just coast into it with the headlights off."

Ron half-smirked as he continued. "Once I'm in the garage, I go to step on the brakes. Wouldn't y'all know it, my foot slips and I end up slammin' down on the gas! That truck went right through the back wall of that garage!" He illustrated the crash with his hands as he spoke.

The men were speechless. Once their shock wore off, they shook their heads, murmuring utterances like "damn" or "Lord, have mercy."

"You know, you're just full of surprises today. I'm guessin' your daddy must've whipped your hide after that nonsense," Coach said to Ron.

"You'd be surprised," Ron started to explain with a sly grin. It had been years since he smiled like that. "Sheww, he cracked the whip on me for a lot of things while growin' up now, but he actually left me off fairly easy with this one."

"No kiddin?" asked Michael, surprised.

Ron nodded. "Mhm. Maybe he was in too much shock, or maybe he was impressed that I even got a date with Martha Lou, I dunno. All he told me was, 'Son, don't get me wrong, I'm mad as all hell at ya, but this is what I'm gonna make you do. You're gonna get a job that's after school and durin' the summer, and you gonna pay for the repair. It don't matter how pretty of a lady you meet, you ain't never gettin' behind the wheel of a vehicle till you're eighteen, or Lord help me.'"

The men couldn't believe how he'd gotten off the hook.

"Aw, man!"

"You lucky dog!"

"You're real fortunate, you know that?" Coach stated. "Must've had an angel watchin' over you. At least when it comes to that young lady you went on a date with, you were respectable about it. I think datin' was a lot better for us than it is for today's generation."

Michael asked, "How you figure?"

"Well, there just seems to be so much silliness. They keep findin' ways to make more drama. It's gotta be exhaustin'! And I'll also just say, it seems like both boys and girls can't keep their eyes from wanderin', you know? None of 'em are faithful to one another."

Michael slapped the table in agreement. "Absolutely agree! It's a growin' problem I've been worried about with this new generation. Matter of fact, even my nephew's son recently got caught two-timin'."

"How old is he?" asked Tony.

"Only sixteen. He goes to school over at Silver Bluff. He's had this one sweetie-pie for almost a year now, if I remember right. He's even brought her around to some of the family things. She's a real sweet gal. Well, a couple months ago, someone on the school's faculty caught him and another young lady skippin' class one afternoon. They were out behind the school smoochin' away. Naturally, word spread quickly down the grapevine to his sweetie-pie. I'm told she was mad as all heck, and honestly, serves him right.

"As one of his elders, I took it upon myself to talk to him a little about it. And y'all know that I ain't perfect now. There's quite a few things I could've done a whole lot better to keep my own wife from separatin', but at least I can say that I was never unfaithful to her. Not once. I don't know how, but that's something the new generation has lost. Feels as if they're all running around cheatin' nowadays. Didn't used to be that way when we were growin' up."

"Mhm," Coach and Ron both said, nodding their heads.

Tony, on the other hand, couldn't help but frown. Something was eating away at him. Turning to Michael, he said, "What're you talking about? Yeah, that definitely happened while we were growing up. Trust me, I've seen it, and… well… I've done it. I've mentioned it to you all before about how my old man had an affair. Running around behind a lady's back, especially when you're young, that's nothing new."

With a condescending shrug, Coach told him, "Well none of us here ever did."

Tony didn't want to let this one go. He was growing more agitated. "Well that's just great, Coach. I'm happy for all of youse guys. Give yourselves a big pat on the back. I'm serious though, don't sit here and act like this is something new. It definitely happened, it was just a hell of a lot more discreet back then. Took years for my old man to get caught."

"How'd that happen, if you don't mind me askin'?" Michael inquired.

Clicking his teeth, Tony responded. "I ratted him out without realizing it."

Coach then asked, "How'd you manage that?"

Tony took a large sip of his coffee before telling the story. "I think I was, um, probably eight or nine. It was a Saturday morning. Dad was out running some errands with my big brothers. I was supposed to be helping Ma out with some stuff around the house, but I think I was more focused on reading my brother's Superman comics. The phone starts ringing. Ma yells, 'Anthony, will you get the phone!' So, I go pick it up. On the other end was a woman asking for my old man. I didn't know who it was, and she wouldn't give me her name, but I could hear that she was crying. Call only lasts for maybe ten seconds before she hangs up. I'm obviously none the wiser, so I tell Ma about it. I don't think much of it, but she starts connecting the dots in her head.

"When my old man gets home, one thing leads to another, they start shouting, and next thing I know, she kicks him out. Later on, my brothers told me that what'd happened was that this lady, who to this day I still don't know the name of, found out that Dad was married with kids. That's what she callin' the house cryin' about."

"Your mama kicked him to the curb, just like that?" asked Coach.

"Just like that." Tony illustrated his point by snapping his fingers. "Growing up became a lot different after that. It really hurt our family. Promised myself that when I had a wife of my own, I wasn't ever gonna make the same mistake. Well, you guys know how good that went. Turns out it's sort of true about the apple not falling far from the tree and all that."

Although he did his best to keep talking in the same humorous, tough tone that he always spoke in, it was easy to hear the disappointment in Tony's voice, along with the guilt in his eyes.

In an effort to lift Tony's spirits, Coach said, "I wouldn't worry all that much about it, Tony. I think you've shown that you try to be a good man, and that's what counts."

Tony shrugged. "Maybe. But if you asked my first wife, she wouldn't say the same thing. Doubt the second one would either. I broke both their hearts all because I wanted more than I had— just like my old man. I don't know about you, but I can't name many other good men who've broken apart their families. Who's grown kids won't talk to him. Who's told not to retire to the same state they live in. Who's kept from seeing their grandkids grow up. Or who's daughter tells them how they don't deserve to be loved by a woman.

"Even to this day, I've never forgiven my father, God rest his soul, for what he did to me and the family. Hell, I hated him for it. Then I go and pull the exact same shit with not just one, but with two different wives. I messed around like I was some sort of big shot, look where it got me. If I'd been a good man, I could be soaking it up on a beach somewhere with a beautiful wife beside me. Instead, I'm right here, an old bachelor in a Hardee's that's long past his prime."

Tony shrugged his shoulders again before taking another sip of his coffee. The other men sat silently with stern expressions on their faces, not really knowing what to say. It wasn't like Tony to ever talk down on himself— in fact, usually the polar opposite— but at the same time, they also felt that he wasn't wrong about what he was saying. Afterall, the men all knew that part of living was living with the consequences of your poor decisions.

Coach finally spoke up. "I don't really know what to tell you, Tony—"

"Ah, don't worry about it," Tony replied. "It is what it is."

Coach continued. "Well, all I can suggest is, maybe you should try forgivin' yourself so you can move on."

Tony brushed Coach's comment off with a wave of his hand. "I'm past that. I've said everything I needed to in confession. What else can you do?"

"You never know, maybe your date tomorrow will be a turnin' point," Michael pointed out.

Since no one had told Coach about the date, he doubled back in surprise. "Oh, you went and got yourself a date! You fixin' to take her to the game tomorrow?"

Tony shook his head with a grin. "Naw, naw. Taking her to the Wilcox."

Coach seemed impressed. "Oh, she sure must be somethin' special."

"Yeah, yeah. We'll see how long she puts up with me."

Coach laughed. "Well I wish you luck with that. You might be missin' out on a good game, though."

"Meh, I think I'll live," Tony snipped back.

"I forgot to mention, I also won't be able to make it tomorrow, Coach," informed Michael.

"What you got goin' on?" Coach asked.

"Oh, I gotta help my sister with some business over in Charleston. Headin' on down that way after this we're done here."

Coach was curiously concerned. "Michael, if you don't mind me askin', is everything alright with your sister?"

With a heavy sigh, Michael began to explain, "Well… I suppose it wouldn't be the worst thing in the world if I told y'all about the matter."

Chapter 5
Properties

In the 1870s, a man named Charles Seele bought 800 acres of land from Solomon Legare, former owner of a Charleston plantation and keeper of enslaved people. The land was a narrow intercoastal island, around two miles from east to west, sitting in the marsh between modern day James Island and Folly Beach. With only a small wooden bridge connecting it to James Island, the land was almost exclusively accessible by boat for a number of years. The vacant wilderness and empty rice fields were inhospitable to most. Mosquitoes brought illnesses such as malaria, and yellow fever plagued the island. Nevertheless, when Seele subdivided the land into small rectangular lots, he sold the lots to a handful of Black farmers: Nelson Left, Edward Green, John Lafayette, and Harrison Wilder.

Though by no means easy, these farmers were able to make a living growing vegetables and fruits on their land while also fishing in the Lowcountry waterways. In 1915, these early farmers, known as the original Sol Legarians, built the Seashore Farmer's Lodge No. 767. The building was not only an economic space for the farmers but also served as a gathering place for the island's growing community. The geographical isolation made it a safe haven for Black and Gullah people looking to escape the predatory Jim Crow laws permeating South Carolina.

In 1922, a Beaufort oyster merchant, George Creighton Varn, leased land from the descendants of Nelson Left in order to create an oyster factory. The lease in question was for a small strip of beach on the south end of the island. The factory brought work to Sol Legarians, as well as many James Islanders and Black residents around the Lowcountry. However, the factory was far from being an ideal place to work. Conditions in and around the factory were dreadful. It was rumored that from over a hundred yards away, you could still smell a reeking fish odor that would cling to your nose for hours.

After Varn's death in 1931, the factory permanently ceased operations, but people colloquially referred to the small strip of beach as "The Factory." The Factory quickly became a new gathering point for the locals. Stores opened where people could buy soul food, adult beverages, listen to the jukebox, play billiards, and share local news. The Factory was one of the six "Black beaches" in the Charleston Lowcountry during the Jim Crow era, further establishing it as a community-hotspot. By 1953, the area was renamed to its current moniker, Mosquito Beach. Once desegregation passed, the area steadily lost visitors as most Black beachgoers opted to forgo the smaller, more mosquito infested beach in favor of Folly Beach.

Michael had been born and raised in Sol Legare and had been lucky to grow up during the area's heyday. None of the three other old men knew the full story about the community, only that Michael had grown up in a historically Black neighborhood surrounding James Island. They didn't have the faintest clue about the humid mornings he spent catching oysters with his dad, the summer evenings playing at Mosquito Beach with his sisters, or the sweet memories of partaking in the neighborhood seafood boils.

Michael began to share with the men at the table. "So, my sister, Dorothy— I'm sure I've told y'all about her before. She still lives in our old family home down in Charleston."

"Is her son the nephew runnin' the garage?" asked Coach.

"No, no, his mama was Evelyn. She was the oldest of the three of us. It goes Evelyn, Dorothy, then me. She probably passed away, um, I think maybe around six years ago now. Anyways, Dorothy's been livin' in that house off and on nearly her whole life. Even when she first moved out when she got married, she was always going back to help out our folks with housework and what not. She usually brought her daughter, Marry, with her. Goin' there always made her happy as a clam. Our folks left it to her before they passed. She's been there ever since—"

Tony rolled his eyes knowing that Michael, like any of these old Southern guys, could ramble your ear off if you weren't careful. In an effort to get him back on course, Tony pointedly asked, "Alright, so… what's going on?"

Surprisingly nonchalant, Michael told them, "She's lost the house."

The air around the table became heavy as the men were taken aback by the news.

Crossing his arms in disbelief, Tony asked, "How could she be losing that house? I mean it's been in your family for Christ knows how long."

With a shrug, Michael simply explained, "She got too behind on her property taxes."

Ron shook his head. "Sheww, that's a tough spot to be in. I know once you get behind on them, that interest adds up quick."

"And that's exactly the problem," Michael stated. "See, her husband, he died back in 2002, he didn't leave her with much. Cost of livin' been risin' for years in Charleston, that includes property taxes. Y'all add a recession on top of all that…"

As Michael trailed off, Ron jumped in to help him finish the train of thought. "It makes for a heap of trouble, don't it?"

The other men all murmured, "Mhm."

Michael continued. "We're livin' through rough times, I tell y'all. Far too many folks' been losin' their homes and jobs. I don't talk about this much, and I ain't gonna dwell on it here, but we've even noticed it at the shop. Things are finally pickin' back up, but they still ain't like they were back in '07. Anyways, I don't mean to—"

Unprompted, Coach interrupted him. "Michael, I'm sorry to butt in, but I got somethin' on my mind that I just gotta ask. It's somethin' I think we're all wonderin'. Now, I don't mean no offense or nothin', but… I'll just say it. If she couldn't afford to pay her bills, why didn't y'all help her out? I mean, you don't just lose your house overnight from not payin' taxes on it."

Tony and Ron leaned away from Coach. Although it was true that they had been wondering about that at the back of their minds, they weren't brazen enough to actually ask. Michael appeared angry at the question, crossing his arms while keeping deadly eye contact with the old lineman.

In a calm but audibly irate voice, he retorted, "Coach, you might not mean no offense, but you sure as the devil are being rude as all shit!" He began to raise his voice without concern for who might hear him. "Lord Almighty, what kind of man do you take me for?"

Without explaining himself, Coach tried to apologize. "Michael, I'm sorry I—"

"Yeah, yeah. You're sorry and what have you." Michael wasn't having it. In a condescending tone, he continued. "Now, I don't mean no offense or nothin', but you should consider thinkin' a little before you make that sort of assumption…" He seemed like he had more to say, but he trailed off, ending with a grunt. "Y'all gettin' on my nerves today. Not that I need to, but just to put y'all's doubts about this whole thing at ease, I would've gladly helped Dorothy," said Michael, dripping with snark. "Matter of fact, I've done it in the past, and I would've done it again. Thing is, she didn't tell me or anyone else about it."

"She never said anything?" Tony asked in disbelief. He didn't doubt what Michael was saying; he was more surprised that Dorothy would let things get this bad.

Michael nodded. "Yes, sir, that's right. She had her reasons for stayin' quiet about it, though I don't agree with any of them. She's been a proud lady, but she sometimes got too much pride for her own good. The last time she came askin' me for help with payin' bills, she promised me that she'd never ask again. Well, little did we know that she meant it.

"Anyways, the point is I ain't rich by no sense, but I've been more fortunate than most in my family. Over the years, I've given them money to help them out when they've needed it." Michael looked Coach dead in the eyes again. "You understand now, don't ya?"

Coach sighed with guilt. "Yes, sir. I hear ya, and I do apologize for what I said. I mean it."

"Thank you." Michael replied. He was far from forgiving, but he was starting to cool off.

Now that the tense moment had passed, Ron asked, "Does your sister got somewhere else she can go?"

"She does. Mary and her husband got an extra room at their house in Ladson. It's gonna be a little cramped in there, especially with Dorothy's grandbaby bein' a teenager, but I think she's excited— no, that's the wrong word. I should say she's *hopeful* about the change."

The other men nodded their heads while grunting "Mhm." Still not ecstatic about the situation, they were glad to hear that there would not be a little old lady left out on the curb with nowhere else to go.

Michael continued to speak his mind. "But yeah, I don't make it on down there much nowadays. Back when my mama and daddy were still alive, they always had everyone over for all the holidays. Fourth of July, Christmas, Thanksgivin', Easter, you name it. Once my sisters were married, they started hostin' at their homes. Their houses were a bit bigger, and if I'm bein' honest with y'all, a fair bit nicer, too."

"I probably haven't visited since…" Michael paused to think. "Sheww, I reckon almost a year. Stopped by to take a look at her car for her around last Veteran's Day. I don't mind visiting the old house every now and then, but I never like stayin' too long. I'll tell y'all, it doesn't feel like the same place anymore, you know? Nowadays, it's different. Can't explain it, just is." He let the thought sit in the open as he took another sip of his coffee. The drink had since become lukewarm.

"What're you fixin' to take from there?" asked Ron.

"Sheww, I'd suppose just this and that. There ain't much of mine that's still there. Maybe an heirloom, or two. I won't lie to y'all, there ain't much there for me to get that I care for. And I know y'all can see that my back ain't what it once was. Dorothy knows that, too. I doubt she thinks I'm gonna find much or be a big help with movin' anything. If you ask me, I reckon she's just tryin' give me one last chance to see where we grew up at. It sure means a whole lot more to her than it does to me."

Tony was astonished by that last bit. "What'd you mean? You don't wanna see your ma's and pop's home?"

"Now, I ain't sayin' that. Don't get me wrong, I'll miss vistin' the place I was raised in. But Dorothy, sheww, it's gonna be real hard for her to move on. I've rambled to y'all before about how I didn't stay there hardly at all after Korea. Served with another Black soldier who promised me he'd get me a mechanic job in Augusta when we got back. As pretty as that little island I grew up on was, and still is, there wasn't much of a future for me there. Well, here I am," he said, pointing at himself. "It's nice to have somewhere with a lot of history to visit, but I've made this town my home a long time ago. I don't regret it.

"Dorothy, on the other hand, Sol Legare is her home, through and through. Between her, Evelyn, and myself, she was always the most in love with it. It's why we didn't argue when our folks said they wanted to leave the house to her. Made the most sense. Honorin' our heritage always been important to her. She's always doin' her darndest to keep our mama's Gullah traditions alive."

Tony asked Michael, "So, do you know who the jackass is that's buying the house?"

"Ha, sure do!" Michael snickered. "Some youngin' who fancies himself as a house flipper, so I'm told."

"Y'all met him?" asked Coach.

"Dorothy did. She only told me about it. He's apparently come around a couple times tryin' to make a deal. Wanted to offer her some money if she moved out earlier than the court was demandin'. I won't lie, it wasn't just some modest sum he was offerin'. I told her, 'You know, Dorothy, if you're havin' to leave anyways, you might wanna take the deal.' Well, she tells me, 'He could offer me all the diamonds and pearls in the world, ain't none of them would be as precious as the time I have left with my home.' Can't say I agree with her line of thinkin', but I can understand."

"And what did she tell him?" asked Tony.

"That he best hit the road!" laughed Michael heartily.

The other men laughed along with him, though nowhere near as robust. Truthfully, they didn't find the story as funny as he did but went along with it anyway for his sake.

Michael continued, "I hate to think what that young man is fixin' on doin' to the property. Come this time next year, it'll be unrecognizable."

"You never know, he might do a good job," Coach said, with a shrug.

"He might. I mean I hope he's able to fix it up nice, don't get me wrong. At the same time, I'd rather he not touch a thing." He let out another groan before continuing. "It's like I said, there's no future in that place for me, but there's a lot of the past he's gonna be buildin' over. A lot of history, a lot of good memories. They're probably all gonna get buried."

Ron shook his head. "Sheww, a damn shame, no matter how you look at it."

"Yes, sir. Look, fellas, I don't really have much else left to say about all this that I haven't already said. This whole thing's been makin' me think a lot, and that's usually not a good thing. it's been makin' me think about how— well, not to be too deep, but how when our time comes, what we leave behind is all that our loved ones will have left of us. Don't get me wrong, I believe I'll be lookin' down on them, but I've come to realize that it's… it's good that they have something of ours that can still get somethin' out of. Hopefully that somethin' gives 'em joy, a helpin' hand, or even a home. It's a gift that keeps on givin'. Y'all get where I'm comin' from?"

"That's right, that's right," said Coach. "I'm sure my babies and grandbabies ain't gonna want any of my football stuff— the wife sure don't want none of it."

The other men roared with laughter.

"Hey now, hey now, y'all didn't hear that. Anyways, Jill and I have already talked about it. We're splitting amongst the kids. Mind y'all, they don't need it. They're way better off than I was at their age. Unlike me, them and their spouses made the smart decision not to work in education. Nonetheless, maybe them or one of the grandbabies might want it. If they decide to sell it, then so be it. Either way, they're gettin' somethin' from us."

Tony pointed at Coach. "That's what I tried to do for my kids. I had a nice four-bedroom house back in Long Island. It was the one I got when I married my second wife. I kept good care of it. When I started thinking about retiring down this way, I kindly asked each of my kids if they would like it. Know what they told me?"

The other men began shaking their heads.

"None of them were interested, none of them! They said I should go ahead, sell the damn thing, and get lost. Believe that?" Tony cursed a bit under his breath.

"I'm a little surprised they didn't want to at least turn around and sell it," said Michael.

"Yeah, I told them that, but they all hate that house. There's too many bad memories there for them. It wasn't worth the trouble for them. Ay, ay, ay. But hey, what can you do? At least it sounds like you got some good memories at your place."

A big grin popped onto Michael's face. "Lord, I sure do… I sure do. I got one comin' to my mind right now that y'all probably get a kick out of."

Chapter 6
Glory Days

"It might not look like much these days, but Mosquito Beach used to be the place to be," Michael began.

"Yeah, sounds like a real paradise," said Tony, sarcastically.

Michael glossed over the joke. "Well, it definitely didn't get that name for no reason now. They love bitin' folks out there on that marsh. But I'll tell y'all, as rough as it was, I still got fond memories of it."

"I'm surprised you just didn't get on over to Folly Beach. It's just up the road from y'all, right?" asked Coach.

"I'm sure we would've if we could. Thing was, unless it was for work, they didn't allow Black folks on Folly till a lot later in the '60s."

The men uttered sentiments like "That's a shame" and "No kiddin'?" often forgetting how different Michael's upbringing had been from their own. Being born with complete freedom of movement was a right they took for granted.

Michael continued with his story. "So, when I was fifteen-years-old, my friends and I were out on Mosquito Beach one late summer afternoon. Lordy, I don't know how, but I can still remember this story like it was yesterday. We were out havin' a good ol' time. All day, we had our eye on this one girl our age, Connie Griffin." Michael smiled as he sighed longingly. "Golly, she was a real looker. She could make a young man wild. She and her family lived over in North Charleston, but they were regulars at the beach. Every young man there knew who she was.

"Now obviously, my buddies and I have been tryin' to get her attention all day. Mind you, we were competing with all the other young men our age, and she had her three older brothers keepin' guard. There finally comes a moment near sundown when they all take a dip in the water, leavin' her by her lonesome. She starts givin' some glances over to us." He started chuckling as he continued. "We're all over the moon that she wants to talk to one of us, but we're all too nervous. We start tellin' each other 'you go over there,' 'no, you talk to her.'"

Laughing along with Michael, Coach chimes in, "I think I see where this is goin'."

"Needless to say, I'm the one who man's up and goes on over to her. I sit next to her on the bank. I make my voice a bit lower when I introduced myself—" Michael stopped to clear his throat. In a half octave lower, he impersonated his younger self. "How do you do, Miss Griffin? My name is Michael." His voice returned back to normal. "And she tells me, much to my surprise, 'I know who you are. I've had my eye on you.'"

"Wheww!" the men said in unison. Even reserved Ron was starting to engage more with the story.

"Now, I'm bein' a proper young gentleman the whole time I'm talkin'. I'm not bein' too forward or nothin', just takin' it nice and slow. By this time, her brothers start noticin' us, and they ain't lookin' too happy with me. I ask little Miss Connie if I can take her on a date sometime. Not only does she tell me yes, she surprises me with a kiss!"

"Well alright now!" His audience loudly applauded him.

Michael motioned his hand downwards, gesturing to the men to settle down. "I know, I know, but trust me, this ain't the end of the story. Now, I'm obviously tickled pink that Connie Griffin just gave me my first kiss. Y'all know, I'm speechless. I start hearing my buddies shoutin' from where they were. I know they've been watchin' me the whole time, so I think they're just rootin' for me. I turn around to them, and I see they're not rootin' for me. They're tryin' to warn me to start runnin, because out of the water,

Connie's brothers are marchin' up to me! I quickly give her my farewells, hopin' to see her again soon, and start runnin' home!"

The men got a real kick out of the story.

Still laughing while talking, Michael pushed on. "Y'all gotta understand, our house is about a good mile and a half away from the beach. There wasn't a single yard between the two where those boys slowed down. Once I started gettin' close to the house, I realize that ain't gonna stop them. They're either gonna barge on in, or I'm gonna get in trouble with my daddy. It's a lose-lose situation. So, right when I come up to a slight bend in the road where they lose sight of me for a single moment, I jump down into the weeds of a creek! I lie down in the water, tryin' be as quiet as can be. Sure enough, they pass me by. I thought I was scot-free now. However, I get home, and my mama sees all my clothes covered in murky creek water. She gave me all manner of heck for that!

"But I tell y'all what, I had the biggest smile on my face the whole time. That's probably one of my favorite stories from growin' up on that island. It's definitely a memory I have from growin' up that I hope I'll never forget."

Tony told him, "You never want to forget your younger days, none of us do."

"Yes sir, yes sir," they all murmured back.

Tony cleared his throat. "Yeah, I miss being wild and young, too."

Coach chimed in, "Well, it's not just about our younger days. Believe me, those weren't always good. The best days of your life can come at any time. It's the stories from those days that are the ones worth rememberin'. The stories that you never get tired of tellin', even when the folks around you are sick of 'em."

Ron finally spoke up. "If you ask me, that sounds like what Rick used to do. Y'all remember how he always had a handful of stories that he always told over, and over, and over."

That other men smiled in fond remembrance. "Oh, right… he sure did," they all murmured, in some form or another.

"Mhm, I tell y'all what, when most men get our age, they tend to tell you one of a few things from their younger days," Coach added. "Either they'll tell you about the trouble they got away with, the pretty women they had, the pretty women they slipped up with, or their regrets. Rick, on the other hand, all the stories he always told us were about his family. I ain't sayin' he didn't get up to no trouble or reckless fun when he was a kid, but those times weren't as important to him as bein' a family man."

Michael nodded in agreement. "First time I actually had a… you know, an actual conversation with him, I noticed right away that his wife and daughters were the stars of the show. I gotta say, as annoyin' as he got sometimes, at the end of the day, all I can say is that he was a lucky man. Not everyone is as fortunate as him in regards to how close they are to their wife and babies."

"That's right now!" Ron and Coach both said together.

Tony snickered. "Yeah, sort of reminds me of this one time. I usually like to talk about my wilder days, but I got one that really gets on my kids' nerves, and I don't think I ever told it to you guys." He sat up in the booth before telling them more. "One time we— actually let me give you guys some background. A few months before my old man got caught two-timing on my ma, he woke my brothers and I up before the crack of dawn one Saturday morning. Tell us to get up, get dressed. Now, we're all saying, you know, 'what gives?' and he says, 'I got a surprise for the three of youse down at *the dock*.' Doesn't say anything else except to pack a jacket. Even as a kid, I knew that was complete bullshit.

"You see, all my brothers and I learned from a young age that *the dock* always meant the one he went to for his business," alluded Tony. "That meant an hour and a half long drive over to this little town on the eastern tip of Long Island called Greenport. Every now and then, he'd take us there with him so we can, as he'd put it, 'start learning the business early.' Man, we always hated it. He would have us out there at four in the morning. It'd still be pitch black outside, shit, we'd be falling asleep standing up, and he'd make us listen about how to tell a good catch from a bad—believe that?

"On this particular morning, we get there, and we drag ourselves out of the car. We're standing there wondering what the lesson is gonna be today… Much to our surprise, the captain of one of the boats yells for us to all get on board. Turns out the day's lesson is actually us going deep sea fishing.

"Wouldn't you know it, we're suddenly wide awake because we're on this man's boat going twenty to thirty miles offshore. It was the first time that any of us had ever been out that far. When you're a kid, that type of thing feels like a big adventure, you know what I'm saying?" Tony kept explaining. "Time comes for us to fish. First the captain showed us how he dragged a net, got the fish in the boat, yada yada. It's interesting to see and all, but I mean, we're kids. We didn't want to sit and watch a lesson. All we wanted was our fishing poles in hand. Luckily, my dad had packed some, so we got cast out off the sides of the boat."

"Y'all catch much?" Coach asked.

Tony's eyes grew wide. "Oh, yeah! Like you wouldn't believe. We couldn't reel those bastards in quick enough. I'll mention that out of my brothers and old man, I'm the one who had the biggest catch of the day."

"No kiddin'?" Ron asked with a hint of skepticism.

"Little eight-year-old me managed to hook a grouper. Shit, it was so big that my old man had to rush over to help me pull it in. Ended up weighing in at thirty-two— thirty-three pounds."

Michael noted to everyone, "I'm sure that fish gets a bit heavier every time you talk about it."

The other men couldn't help but laugh.

Tony smirked back at the men. "Alright, alright, you wise guys always get on my nerves, I swear. As I was saying, I caught the biggest fish of the day. Can't tell you guys how great it was to rub my big brothers' faces in it. Man, it was great! It got even better on the way back because they both got seasick, but I didn't. Being a little kid and seeing your two older brothers puking their guts out over the rails of a boat— couldn't ask for a better time!"

"Now, did you do the same thing with your kids?" inquired Coach.

"Mhm," Tony muttered while taking a sip of coffee. At this point, his cup was close to being empty. "Did nearly the exact same thing. Woke them up real early, told them there was surprise, all that stuff. Just like I'd been, kids went from hating my guts to being over the moon once we set off on the boat. The day was real good. Was the kinda day that really makes you like being a dad. I know my old man brought my brothers and I out there to mainly give us some perspective on where our money comes from, but I like to think he was doing it because he saw that we had fun. I enjoyed sharing that experience with my kids, too. Makes you feel like a real family man."

"Mhm, that's right," the other men agreed, quietly reflecting on Tony's story for a moment.

After a few seconds, Tony added, "Anyways, I like talking about that trip. Had a feeling you guys would appreciate it." He stopped to sigh, wistfully. "I wish my kids did. Whenever I try to talk to them about it, they just roll their eyes. At least, that's what they do when they actually talk to me. Well, what can you do, you know? What can you do?"

Coach knew that Tony mentioning the issues with his kids would quickly sour the good mood at the booth, so he decided to tactfully redirect the conversation.

Clearing his throat, Coach exclaimed, "Yeah, I tell y'all, I've had a blessed and fulfillin' life. Back when I was a young man, I thought that nothin' in my life was gonna top me making touchdown off a fumble for Georgia. I think for a lot of other men, that may very well might be the case. Can't say I blame them. Then right after I finished school, I married Jill, and I'll admit it, that topped that touchdown. Felt that way about it back then, still feel the same about it now." He paused to laugh at himself before saying, "Although Jill might say it's become her biggest regret."

The other men joined in with his laughter.

"O'Lordy. Well, um, a year or two later we had our baby girl, Kathy. Not too soon, Daniel came along, too. Becomin' a father… sheww, that's somethin' else. Everything I did before that suddenly felt a whole lot smaller. Your whole world changes when you have a kid. Changes even more when you have another one."

"Yes, sir. That's right," his small audience concurred.

"Tony, that fishin' trip of yours reminds me of this one trip I took Danny on," Coach remarked. "Jill and I took the kids over to Knoxville at the start of the summer vacation one year. This was before Pigeon Forge was known outside of Tennessee, so that's the city Jill and I grew up goin' to when we wanted to get out to the Smokies."

"That's how it was back before Miss Dolly Parton came along. She put that town on the map," noted Ron.

Coach nodded his head. "I tell y'all what, she sure did. She created a lot of jobs for folks over there. Only complaint I got is the amount of folks vistin'. Now there's hardly any room out on the water to fish! I haven't been there in five years, and I don't have any plans to, given my hip, but I'm sure it's even more crowded now…

"Anyways, I apologize to y'all. There I go ramblin' on another tangent." Coach shifted back to his original story. "As I was startin' to say, we went to Knoxville for vacation one year. I thought it'd be nice to let the girls run off to do whatever in town while Danny and I do something together, just somethin' for us boys. I arranged for us to rent a canoe closer to Asheville so we could paddle down the French Broad for a few miles. He'd obviously been on a boat before, but he'd never gone down an actual river on a canoe before. I thought he'd get a real kick out of it.

"So, we got up real early that mornin', and we drove an hour or so over to the boat rental place. One of the men there drove us and our canoe up closer to Asheville. So, we get to a paddlin' on the water, and Danny is havin' the time of his life! He's got the biggest smile on his face goin' from ear to ear. After about two miles, we come up on our first really tall bridge that's crossing between two cliffs. There ain't too many cars passin' over on it, but what was really neat was that there no barrier or nothin' keepin' you from the support beam.

"I have the canoe go right up next to the beam, and Danny is able to reach out and actually touch it with his hand. And you know, he's just at a lost for words. He's lookin' up, down, and all around at all the steel around him. We finish passing under the bridge, then he turns around to me, his eyes are all big, and he just goes, 'Dad, this is so cool!'"

Coach went silent for a moment, savoring the happy memory. "I always say, I'll never forget that moment. It's times like those you really appreciate bein' a dad."

"Sounds like a heck of a trip," Ron remarked.

Coach laughed. "Well, it did have its hiccups now. A little ways after that bridge, we came around to this bend that had a fairly wide bank. Some college kids, at least I reckon they were around that age, were cookin' out and drinkin'. Drinkin' a *whole* lot. Them boys and girls were being loud as all heck, hootin' and hollerin' at one another. Mind you, this is back in the 70s, so I wasn't expectin' any of this out that way. So as we were coming around the bend, this one young man yells to this one pretty young lady something along the lines of, 'I thought you said you were gonna show me somethin'.' This lady lifts up her tank top to flash the whole lot of 'em! Obviously, Danny and I both see this happenin'. I'm just there thinkin' to myself how this lady unknowingly just exposed herself to my eleven-year-old."

Tony dryly cracked a joke. "Better that than a dirty magazine, you know what I'm saying?"

Coach brushed the comment off. "Sure, sure. Anyways, after they're behind us, I tell him, 'Danny, you're not in trouble for seein' that. Main thing is, whatever you do… don't tell your mama!'"

The men laughed at the story's epic conclusion. "Ah, shoot. I tell you what, that's the truth right there," they all spoke in some form or another.

As the laughter died down, once again sat in silence for a few moments. Their coffees— what was left— had long lost their heat and were now little more than bitter water. Out of habit, the men continued to finish what they had left in their cups. Ron took this time to stare out the window in the direction of his truck, not thinking about anything in particular.

Coach noticed Ron looking at the old Chevy. He asked, "Your truck still runnin' good?"

Without turning away from the window, Ron grumbled, "Mhm."

"Nothing's gonna stop that truck, as long as you don't go ramming it through any garages," added Tony sarcastically, calling back to the story Ron shared earlier.

The table uproared in laughter, and even Ron let out a chuckle.

Throughout the morning, Michael had noticed that Ron was unusually silent and decided to try to rope him back into being an active participant in the conversation. "Ron, you've been quiet this mornin'. You didn't mention what kinda trips you've been on, or the trouble you got into when you were a youngin'."

Ron turned his attention back to the table, coughing. After clearing his throat, he offered, "Well, y'all heard about my little joyride. Ain't much else to tell. I was never one for gettin' into much trouble. Suppose you could say I wanted to stay on the straight and narrow."

"Oh, come on, Ron!" Tony clapped back. "We're all guys here. You can't sit here and tell us that you didn't ever have wild oats when you were a young man."

"Y'all got understand, I didn't get to be a young man for long. Right after high school, I was off fighting in the Pacific…"

At the mention of that time, memories that Ron hadn't thought of in years came flooding back. There were many from that time that he never cared to remember— he could still remember the faces of the friends he made while serving in the campaign, many who had been younger than him, practically still boys. He could still remember the brotherly bonds they formed with one another on the Islands, the way they leaned on one another for support during an arduous time. And Ron could distinctly remember how each of these young men met their untimely, gruesome end: gunned down, maimed by enemy attacks, and blown up on the beaches of islands that he had never known existed before then.

Ron did his best to compose himself, suppressing those harrowing images to the dark recesses of his mind. "I, um… here's what I can say." He stopped to loudly cough twice to then revisit the original question. "If y'all ask me, the best times in my life started when I got back home from servin'. Without droppin' off my gear and bags, I went straight to the jeweler, then right to Betty's. Soon as she opened the door, I asked her to be my wife. When I look back, I can say that was the first day of what would become the best days of my life. They got even better once Patsy came along."

"That sure sounds nice." Coach said to Ron. He then turned to Michael and Tony. "Fellas, don't that sound good?"

Michael nodded his head, "Mhm, sure do."

Ron raised an eyebrow at their reaction. Something felt off; the words felt forced.

Before Ron could question the men's motives, Tony asked, "You still talk to your daughter?"

The question caused Ron to tilt his head in confusion. "I do. I mean, maybe not as much as I should, but—"

Tony continued to talk over Ron. "Yeah, you're lucky, you know? Still got a daughter that loves you. Gotta be tough being this far away from one another."

Before Ron could get a word in edgewise, Michael added, "And I know she got that grandbaby of yours. I'm sure the kid would love seeing his grandpa a little more."

Coach was about to add his two cents to the conversation when Ron began shouting "Dagnabbit! What in the *blazes* are y'all doin?" He shook his head aggressively while cursing fiercely under his breath. He frilled his brow and scowled, highlighting the wrinkles all around his mouth. "Lord, have mercy. Since when were y'all so concerned with meddlin' in my business?"

The three other men exchanged silent glances with one another, deciding which one of them needed to bite the bullet.

After some moments of wordless deliberation, Coach finally volunteered. He cleared his throat as he searched for the right words. "Ron… this is somethin' we ain't got much right to meddle in… ah, shoot. Look, we need to talk to you about somethin'."

Chapter 7
Farewells

"Well, get on with it! I ain't got all day," Ron spat back.

Coach took a deep breath before continuing. "Alright, I'll just get straight to the point. Ron, we've all been talking about this for a while, and that also includes Rick. We think the time's come for you to really consider livin' with your daughter, or at least movin' up there to be closer to her."

Ron seethed, thinking the men were out of their damn minds. "Y'all think I should move in with her? In *Connecticut?*"

Tony explained, "You'd like that part of the state, Ron. Trust me, it wouldn't feel all that different from Aiken."

"Now y'all wait a dang minute! I ain't goin' nowhere. This here is my *home!*"

Ron felt himself getting more heated by the second. Hearing this kind of talk come from his daughter was one thing, but he felt it was entirely inappropriate for these men to even mention the idea, especially in a public setting. He thought this little coffee meetup was the one place where he was still seen as just another man, not as a bag of bones that couldn't take care of himself. Coach could see that Ron was getting upset. He didn't like having to give this talk— Rick would have been a lot better at this sort of thing.

Despite Ron's resistance Coach did his best to keep speaking in a jolly demeanor. "I know you don't like hearing this, but your health ain't what it used to be. You've been real fortunate with your old age, we ain't denyin' that. However... we've been, uh, noticin' a real decline."

If it wouldn't have been perceived as rude, Ron would have spat on the ground at the insulting explanation. Scowling, he said to all of them, "Is that the problem y'all have, huh? Think I ain't fully capable of takin' care of myself? Look here, I don't need *nobody* babysittin' me. I've been on my lonesome for Lord knows how many years, and I don't intend on changin' now."

Coach was beginning to lose his patience and couldn't help raising his voice a little at Ron in his reply. "Well, that right there is the problem. If you keep this up, you ain't gonna get another year. For all we know, you might take someone else with you, given how you've been drivin' your truck lately."

That comment surprised Ron. "My drivin'? Sheww, there ain't nothin' wrong with my drivin'. I can still see perfectly fine, and I got me a mind of an ox."

"No, you don't," said Michael, sternly. "I've been drivin' right behind ya when you're at the wheel. I don't mean no offense, but I gotta be honest, it wasn't pretty."

"This is ridiculous! I didn't get up this mornin' just to come get talked down to by y'all!" Ron exclaimed, feeling attacked by the friends he once trusted.

Coach strained to keep his voice down. "We ain't talkin' down to ya. We're only tryin' to help you."

"Help me! I don't *need* no help!" Ron could feel his blood pressure rising dangerously high, so he took a second to calm himself down. After two deep breaths, he asked, "How long have y'all been talkin' about this behind my back for, huh?"

The three men were apprehensive, shrugging their shoulders as they struggled to answer.

Finally, a frustrated Tony clicked his teeth and confessed. "You know what? It doesn't matter. Sooner or later, you'd find out anyway. Your daughter's the one who called Rick, okay? She asked him to try talking some sense into that thick skull of yours. Then he came to us asking for our help. We'd planned to talk to you about it today, but… well, that tragic fucking thing happened with Rick, God rest his soul."

Ron shook his head in disbelief while looking down at the table. "Outrageous, simply outrageous," he muttered to himself. He looked back up at the men. "Patsy should've never gotten y'all involved. I've known y'all for years now, but that don't give none of y'all the right to tell me that I should leave my home."

Now annoyed, Michael asked, "Why do you consider this place to be your home?"

Ron thought the question was asinine. "*Why?* For cryin' out loud, I've lived here for Lord knows how long! I got my house here, raised my baby here, spent the best years of my life here."

Michael stiffly replied, "And those times are over. There ain't nothin' here for you anymore. You spend all day, every day, by your lonesome. You've told me before how you haven't been to church in years. I reckon this little thing in the mornin' is the only time you ever get out with other folks—"

"Now that ain't true!"

Michael continued. "No, Ron. It is… it is. We all know it. You ain't slick. And look here, I hope you have many years left, but what you're doin' right now… frankly, you're wastin' the rest of the time you've been given."

With a foul look still painted on his face, Ron could only shake his head at that explanation. "That's big talk comin' from you. Only a little bit ago, you were makin' fuss about how your sister is losin' y'all's family's house."

Using the house as a counterpoint struck a nerve with Michael. "You think that you have the right to compare yourself to what's happenin' to my sister? Lordy, your mind might be goin' quicker than I thought. Unlike you, my sister was born in that home. Unlike you, she is movin' in with her daughter's family. And also, unlike *you*," Michael concluded, dripping with disdain, "she's doin' it with her head held high."

At this point, Michael and Ron were both furious, angrily boring their eyes into one another. Both wanted to ream the other out but neither wanted to say something they would ultimately regret in the heat of the moment.

Coach butted in. "Alright, you two. That's enough. Ron, Michael's got a point. We like havin' you, but there ain't much here for ya. You still got yourself a family that loves ya. I hate to be this blunt, but you should spend the time you've been given with them."

Tony tried to say something to support Coach's reasoning, but Ron stopped paying attention. All of their words were muffled by the fury ringing in his head. He'd reached his limit.

Petulant, he shut up whoever was talking by aggressively banging on the table with his palm. "That is *it*! I've sat here all morning, listenin' to all of y'all's crap, and I've had about all I'm gonna take. I shouldn't have to explain myself, but I'm gonna say what I gotta say. When y'all get to my age, y'all will understand. It is terrible, terrible, to live longer than your friends… your wife. Don't see much of a point anymore of meetin' anyone else. If I don't go first, it's gonna be them, and I don't wanna go to anymore damn funerals.

"And *don't* tell me how I still got a daughter. Believe me, I'd love to be closer to her, but I ain't gonna be a burden to her. If she wants to help take care of me, that's what would happen. I'd stop bein' her daddy and start bein' the grown man who can't take care of himself. That ain't no way to live. If you ask me, I'd rather be six feet under before I ever let that happen."

With a disappointed sigh, Coach responded, "So is that it? You gonna be an old hermit until you pass away? That ain't no way to live your life."

Ron looked Coach dead in the eye. "Well, you don't got nothin' to worry about because it don't concern you. Now if you'd please excuse me, I'd think I better be off."

Coach didn't scoot out of the booth right away to let the cranky man out, still trying to reason with him. "Ron, come on now—"

Ron snapped, "Coach, I don't wanna ask you again. Now, move."

Frustrated, Coach begrudgingly pulled himself out of the booth. Ron took one last sip of his cold coffee, grabbed his cane, and slid out leaving the newspaper he had been reading on the table. He walked to the front door of the Hardee's without stopping to say goodbye. From the window by the table, the other men watched him walk across the parking lot to his truck.

"Damn…" Tony groaned. "What are you gonna do, you know? We tried."

"He's mighty stubborn, Lord forgive him," said Michael, shaking his head with defeat.

They watched as Ron struggled to get into the driver seat of his Chevy.

"Yep, that might've been more trouble than it was worth," Coach surmised. "It probably would've gone better if Rick had been here, but you gotta play the cards that the Lord deals ya."

"Mhm," Michael and Tony agreed.

Ron drove his truck out of the parking lot. Sure enough, he almost caused an accident while making a right turn onto Whiskey Road.

"You guys see that? The nerve on that guy. Unbelievable!" exclaimed Tony. "After all this, we'll see if he even shows up next week. What do the two of youse think?"

Michael answered earnestly, "I wouldn't worry about it. I reckon he'll still come back."

"Agreed," said Coach.

"Yeah? How do youse figure?" asked Tony.

Michael shrugged matter-of-factly. "Because where else is he gonna go?"

The three men sat silently at the table. The only sounds were the humming of the fluorescent lights, the clanking of metal from the kitchen, and the groans that the old men's congested breathing created in the space. Frankly, the whole ordeal had left them feeling exhausted— it was impressive the toll that one cranky old man could have on a group. Besides, having to hold an intervention, for lack of a better term, was certainly not one of their strong suits.

After a few minutes, Michael cleared his throat. "Well, fellas, I suppose I should start fixin' to get on the road. I have a busy weekend ahead of me."

Coach and Tony both muttered, "Oh, yeah, yeah, of course..."

Michael turned to the Long Islander sitting next to him. "Tony, I hope all goes well with that pretty lady of yours tomorrow," he said with a wink.

Coach laughed. "Oh, buddy! You got your work cut out for you tomorrow."

"Yeah, alright, taking a woman out to dinner is nothing I can't handle. You, on the other hand, got yourself the most important game of the season to win."

Coach nodded. "Yes, sir. Yes, sir. Those boys and I will need all the luck we can get."

"Ah, well don't you worry. Most of the folks on this side of town, and myself, we'll all be prayin' for y'all." Michael said as he began to slide out of the booth.

As Coach stood up, using his cane, he said, "And Michael, I wanna say again that I'm sorry for what I said earlier, and also for everything that's happen' with your sister. It's a… it's an awful thing to have happen to anyone, but especially someone her age."

"Well, I do appreciate you sayin' that, Coach. I really do. Before I forget, let me know when you hear more about when Rick's funeral will happen."

"Yeah, let me know, too," added Tony. He slid out of the booth to stand alongside the other two men.

"Absolutely, will do." After a couple of seconds of silence between the three of them, Coach said, "Well, I got business to get done before practice today. Y'all take care now." He reached out to shake their hands.

"I'll see youse around," said Tony.

After they all shook hands, Tony and Coach walked to the front door while Michael headed to the bathroom.

Without stopping to turn around fully, Michael gave them both a wave. "Y'all be good."

Chapter 8
Whittle Away the Days

After leaving Hardee's in a huff, Ron drove over to the other side of town, parking in a handicap spot outside of Wal-Mart. For the last twenty minutes, he had done nothing but fester in his car. With no one else around to hear, he was whispering all manner of foul curses. He had not been this mad in a very long time, and it had been even longer since he felt so disrespected. What gave these men the right to decide whether Ron could take care of himself or not?

Although Ron assumed that no one could notice him talking to himself, he was oblivious to the small scene he was making. People walking by stared at the old man having a meltdown in his truck, watching partially out of concern but mainly out of morbid curiosity. Some of the passersby thought about tapping on the window to see if the man needed help. In the end, though, they all decided not to get involved in a stranger's business.

What finally got Ron out of his rage-induced trance was when he punched the steering wheel. Instead of aiming for its soft middle, he hit the hard right side of the device, causing a sharp stab of pain to shoot through his right hand.

"Dagnabbit!" he shouted while clenching his injured fist with his other hand.

The sharp throbbing made him wince, feeling like hundreds of tiny needles in his knuckles and fingers. There was no good reason for him, or anyone for that matter, to have punched the steering wheel, especially with a hand riddled with arthritis. Once the pain began to subside, Ron made sure that he could still move all his stiff fingers. Thankfully his hand wasn't broken, but it was definitely going to be bruised for the next several days.

Ron realized this was a sign for him to calm his rage. Besides, nothing good was coming out of his little tantrum. While focusing on slowing down his breathing, he looked at the time on his watch— almost eight o'clock. Composing himself, he opened the glove box. The compartment held a neatly folded blue vest and a plastic name badge; Ron took out both items. He then turned off the engine, put the keys in his pocket, took his cane off the passenger seat, and stepped out of the Chevy to walk across the parking lot, and into the Wal-Mart. It was almost time for his shift.

The recession that began in 2008 was merciless to many. Despite being retired for three decades, Ron found himself a victim of the unforeseen economic downturn. A large chunk of his savings and small pension were lost when the market went down, and while he was still better off than most in his position, he still needed a little extra to get by.

Without telling any friends or family, he was able to scrounge up extra income as a Wal-Mart greeter. Reentering the workforce had never been his plan— picturing himself working at the chain store had never crossed his mind— but when push came to shove, Wal-Mart was the only place in town willing to hire someone of his age.

This morning, Ron's coworkers noticed him walk in but none of them, not even the ones close to his age, acknowledged him. They used to attempt to greet him with warm smiles, but he returned their warm gestures only with scowls, garnering the reputation as the store's mean old man. His coworkers didn't understand why Ron was the way he was since they only ever extended him kindness, but that wasn't how Ron saw it.

From the start of his employment, Ron could tell that they didn't think of him as just another coworker. For starters, they always spoke to him differently than how they did with each other; everyone talked slowly to him in an over-friendly tone, almost like a child, and they acted like everything he did was some huge achievement. Ron quickly realized that his coworkers all thought of him as the old, pitiful, charity hire— not as another working man which irritated him to no end. He acknowledged that they were trying to be nice, but that fact didn't make it hurt any less. He was already ashamed and embarrassed enough to be back in the workforce, and their good intentions only added salt on his already wounded pride.

On his way to the breakroom to clock in, Ron saw his manager, Tina, glued to her phone texting someone. She was in her late twenties. Back at the factory, he was no stranger to having managers and supervisors that were younger than him but never to this extent. He always thought that it strange how she was young enough to be his granddaughter. Once she finally took a break from her text conversation, she noticed him.

"Good mornin', Ron," she said before going back to the business on her phone.

Instead of waving back at her, Ron simply lifted up his hand to acknowledge her. "Good morning, Miss Tina."

Without lifting her face up from the screen, she instructed, "I'm gonna have you begin greeting at the north door. After your lunch, you'll be on receipt checkin'."

Ron cleared his throat. "Yes, ma'am." Not once did she stop to look up from her phone at him as he walked by. She knew from the experience that there was no hope of having a good conversation with him.

After Ron put on his uniform and clocked in, he took his position at the main entrance. He stood at attention, putting on a fake smile to welcome customers. People coming into the store were often concerned about why an old man with a cane was being forced to stand for hours when he actually didn't have to. Managers were always offering him a stool to sit on or even permission to use one of the store's electric scooters, but he was always adamantly against the idea. This poorly thought-out decision always left Ron exhausted and sore by the end of his shift, but he was too stubborn to accept any form of assistance.

This particular workday went about like any other— nothing remarkable to note. Everyone who entered the store greeted him back, and when he got to checking receipts, every customer complied with his request to quickly eye their cart of items. Per usual, the hardest part about his job was how it tended to be mind-numbingly mundane. Then again, at least this job got him out of the house. Ron still couldn't decide which was worse: waiting for his shift to be over or waiting at home for the day to be over.

Around 3:30, he only had thirty more minutes left on the clock. While handing a receipt back to a nice young mother with her infant, his heart sank when he looked over at the checkout lines: Coach was at a register buying a few packets of sports drink powder mix. Ron wasn't sure if his coffee acquaintance had noticed him yet, curious as to why the man was over on this side of town. The main reason Ron worked at this location, instead of the Wal-Mart on his side of town, was so that none of his peers would find out about his little secret.

Ron continued in horror as Coach finished checking out and began walking towards him. He wished he could keep his head down to avoid the judgmental stare that he assumed he would get from Coach but he knew that wasn't the proper thing to do. It was his job, both as an employee and as a man, to have the decency to look another man in the eye.

Coach looked confused when he finally noticed Ron in uniform. He momentarily thought maybe his mind was starting to go, but sure enough, that was his friend standing there. Coach had no idea that Ron was working, although he had suspected for a while that money was tighter for the old man than he let on and it appeared that he was right. He could tell that Ron, to put it lightly, wasn't pleased to see him— the embarrassment was all too visible on the senior's face. Coach thought about striking up a brief conversation with Ron, but his instincts told him to do otherwise. He figured that the better move was to preserve any remaining shred of the man's fragile dignity.

When Coach walked up to him, Ron didn't have to ask him for his receipt— Coach already had it out and ready to go.

"Good afternoon, sir," Coach said while handing Ron the receipt. He held the plastic open that contained the powder packets. "I ain't got too much here."

Ron was pleasantly surprised that Coach didn't say anything else about the situation. It didn't ease his feeling of shame— there was little that could— but the encounter was at least more bearable this way. Ron peered into the plastic bag to appear as though he was checking what was in there. For all he cared, Coach could've been shoplifting an entire television, and he wouldn't have said a word; Ron only wanted him out of his workplace. Ron looked up from the bag at Coach. The old football star tried to keep a cheery smile on his face, but he couldn't hide the look in his eyes— a look of pity.

Releasing a heavy groan, Ron told Coach, "Thank you, sir. You have a good rest of your day now."

Coach silently nodded for a few seconds. He wondered if he should say more, but ultimately decided not to. The silence between the two of them had already said enough.

"You as well. You take care of yourself," Coach replied.

When Coach finally walked away, Ron finally breathed a sigh of relief. The last thing Ron wanted was for people to know about his situation, and he definitely didn't want word getting back to Patsy about it. If she knew, he wouldn't hear the end of it. Something about the awkwardness of this interaction with Coach made him feel like there was no need to worry. He knew that the man, the same one that he had yelled at earlier that morning, would keep all of this a secret. He was thankful for that.

***

Fifteen minutes later, Ron was given permission to clock out. He left without telling any of his coworkers goodbye, like he always did. Once he was back in his Chevy, he eagerly drove straight home. His house, the same one that he and Betty had bought decades ago, was on Powderhouse Road. The place itself wasn't anything too special and was smaller than most double-wides. The section of driveway right off the road tended to flood whenever it rained, the house's siding was beginning to peel, the yard was overgrown, and the garage door no longer opened— frankly, it was all too much for Ron to keep up with.

Patsy had been telling him for years that he should try selling the old house before deteriorating past the point of no return. If he didn't want to come live with her, she thought, he could at least move into a smaller home. Ron always scoffed at the notion, acting like she was out of her mind at the suggestion.

He turned onto the driveway where a small puddle lingered from the previous night's rain. He parked his truck in front of the inoperable garage door. There were no neighbors to greet him as he walked to the front door, as the other houses on the street were separated by thick bands of pine trees, and the home across the street was almost completely out of view from the main road.

After unlocking the faded red front door, Ron walked inside. He sat his car keys down in a little glass bowl that sat on an end table by the door. One of Betty's self-imposed duties had been to always keep the dish stocked with hard candy and peppermints.

He then walked into the living room to sit in his leather recliner. His usual routine after work was to lounge about on it while watching ESPN, or napping, but as he sat down, he found he was still too shaken up to rest. He was still angry at the men for poking their heads into his business. Then again, perhaps they had a point.

Ron took a second to scan the room. Although he kept the small end table next to his recliner fairly clean, the rest of the living room— and really the whole house— was covered in clutter and caked with dust. He suddenly felt a twinge of guilt for letting things get to this point. He figured Betty would have whipped his hide if she could have seen the way he stacked torn books and crumpled newspapers on the couch.

In a state of restlessness, Ron climbed out of the recliner, walking over to the small kitchen. Bowls of stale cereal crumbs were piled in the sink, and old frozen dinner trays were scattered across the countertops. He opened the fridge to see what was on the menu for dinner tonight but beside a fresh carton of milk, a bottle of barbecue sauce, and a jar of pickles, the refrigerator was empty. He closed the door before moving on to the freezer.

"Lordy," he said to himself, shaking his head.

There were two frozen dinners from Wal-Mart inside. He himself had never learned to cook, so he'd been living off of prepared meals for years. Like any Southern man worth a dime, he used to love making barbecue out on his grill. The problem was that it took a lot of effort— too much effort if he was only feeding himself.

Ron was getting more fed up with himself. Stubborn as ever, the last thing he wanted to do was admit that the men— and Patsy— had told him so. He slammed the freezer door shut, causing the entire refrigerator to shake. He waddled back to the living room, muttering angrily to himself like he had in his truck that same morning. Before sitting back in his recliner, he noticed there was a new message on the old landline by the couch. He didn't particularly care about checking the singular voicemail, but it gave him something to occupy his mind.

As he pressed play, he was greeted by Patsy's voice. Her Southern accent went in and out. *"Hi, Dad, it's me."* She sounded downtrodden. *"I wanted to let you know I heard about Rick. Maggie just called to tell me... I'm sorry to hear about him. I hope you're doin' okay."*

Ron cleared some space on the couch to sit as he listened.

"I know you and mom were great friends of theirs. Everyone was a friend of his." She laughed gently. "I actually spoke to him over the phone a couple days ago. He sounded well. I would've never guessed something like this would happen. One moment you're catchin' up with someone, then they're gone the next... it's an awful feeling.

"If you ever want to talk to someone, you're always welcome to give me a call. I'm only offerin'. I'm not trying to tell you what to do. I know you can't stand it when I do... I'm just... just worried about you, Dad.

Anyways, like I said, I'm sorry about Rick. You're probably out right now, but give me a call later today if you want. I miss you, Dad. Believe me, we all do... You know I love ya. Bye."

Once the message ended, Ron sat in silence. Patsy's message kept replaying in his mind like a broken record. Her words, *"One moment you're catchin' up with someone, then they're gone the next,"* echoed in his head— a sentiment that he was all too familiar with, a fear that had taken control over his life. His brothers in the war, people he called friends, and above all else, Betty, had all left this world, leaving him on his own. Losing them was pain that never stopped weighing on his heart. Despite all of this loss, he still appreciated Patsy giving him a call. For the first time in a long time, her voice brought him comfort.

An idea suddenly popped into his head. Getting up from the couch, he meandered over to the credenza housing his flatscreen T.V. He carefully got down on his knees to open the furniture's double doors.

The item he wanted *had* to be somewhere in its cabinet, at least that's where he remembered Betty always kept it. After shuffling through assorted knickknacks, junk items, old instruction manuals, and spare extension cords, he finally found what he was looking for: a family photo album.

The album was a well-worn Gamecocks-themed binder. Some of the plastic was lifting off the front cover, and the spine was torn, but the inner metal rings still firmly held the many pages of carefully curated pictures. The album was heavy from Betty packing it to the brim, ranging from photos when the two met those many decades ago, all the way up to Patsy's wedding.

Ron tucked the thick binder under his arm. With careful effort, he stood up and, after catching his breath, he brought the album over to his recliner so he could eagerly flip through the pages.

The first picture was one of Betty and Ron having ice cream together. If he remembered correctly, this was their first date. Each with a cone in hand, Betty was giggling at a blushing Ron, who had a smidge of cream on his nose. Lordy, he looked so different now than from how he did back. He almost couldn't believe that the handsome young man in the photo was him. Besides her hairstyle and its color, Betty was still the same beautiful woman that she had always been, even up until the end.

He skimmed through a few more pages: Photos of Ron and Betty each graduating high school; him in his uniform before and after the war; both of them outside of church; Betty showing off her new engagement ring; and finally, their wedding day. It had been ages since he looked at the old wedding photos— Betty looked so gorgeous and *happy*. He still considered himself a lucky man.

He flipped ahead in the album to when Patsy entered the picture. She was born with a full patch of curly hair. She was such a little blessing for the couple; they had been trying to have children for years before she was born but couldn't conceive until Ron and Betty were both in their thirties. Despite these initial challenges, that little baby changed both their lives for the better. After the baby photos came those of Patsy as a toddler, including a couple of shots of her with spaghetti sauce all over her chi which elicited a laugh from Ron. He turned through two more pages, stopping on one in particular that caught his eye.

In this family photo at Lake Bowen, Ron held a smiling four-year-old Patsy while Betty stood next to them with her arm around him lovingly. They were somewhere on the banks of the water, probably visiting his parents for the day. Although he was happy to stumble across this photo of his smiling wife and daughter, what really struck him was seeing his own face. He radiated pure joy and contentment in his eyes. All he needed to be humbly satisfied was a happy wife and daughter— nothing more, nothing less. He missed that long-forgotten feeling.

He thought again about what Coach had told him that morning. "There ain't much here for ya…You should spend the time you've been given with them." Maybe the men had a point; perhaps he really was wasting his sunset years. After all, what was he really doing? When he wasn't working, all he did was sit alone in his living room. Besides the Thursday morning coffee, he never spoke to anyone else— he wasn't exactly living a fulfilling life. At the same time, he found himself wondering whether there was even a point in trying. He feared, as he secretly had for many years, that if he got close to anyone, he would either have to watch them go or worse— watch himself become a burden to them.

Ron took one last look at the lake picture before closing the binder. He suddenly had the urge to do something that he had not done in years. Leaning the photo album against the armrest of the recliner and foregoing his cane, he carefully walked over to the coat closet, nestled in the hallway that led to the bathroom and bedrooms. Like a lot of the storage spaces in his house, he mostly kept old junk in there that he was long overdue to get rid of. He rearranged the rubbish to the side to grab what he was looking for: his old guitar case.

A bit heavier than he remembered, Ron carried the guitar case back into the living room, setting it down in front of the couch as he took his seat. He was pleasantly surprised to see the old steel string acoustic was still in excellent condition, somehow perfectly preserved after all these years. He put the guitar in his lap.

Underneath the guitar, still sitting in the case amongst plastic picks, was a black and white photograph of him and Betty on a date before their wedding. Unlike the pictures in the album that were better protected from the elements, this photo was heavily faded with a distinctive orange hue. It had been a long time since Ron had seen this particular photo, a personal favorite. The two of them sat at a picnic table, each holding a Coke bottle, and gazing lovingly at one another.

Ron looked longingly at the photo as he tuned the guitar. He made sure to be careful so as not to make the old strings snap. Once he was satisfied with the sound, he grabbed one of the old picks from the case and tried putting his fingers on the strings. At his age, he found it difficult to bend his stiff joints the way he wanted, but in the end, he found that he still had enough finesse to play different chords.

He decided to play a folk song he wrote when he returned home from the war— one that was what he imagined growing old might be like. He anticipated that he wouldn't remember any of the chords or even a single note, but like muscle memory his hands still knew where to go. As he finally got the hang of it, he couldn't help but imagine that Betty was there with him on the couch, listening along to his tune as she often had in the past.

He sang:

I've gone from my old family's home
Left a Southern town while I'm still young
Don't got much money to my name
But I got the holy spirit in my heart

Fought on islands you've never known
Ran on beaches with lead in my lungs
Sailed from Okinawa for my girl
Lord knows she always got my heart

Many good long years have come and gone
My woman can barely stand me no more
But I made a promise on the altar
And best believe I'll see it through

When my hair is gray, and I got sore bones
I hope and pray you don't walk out that door
Happiness only lives when I'm with you
Oh, I wanna stay with you till our lives are through

Now I'm sitting on a front porch all alone
Remeberin' my days as a sprout young man
Still thinkin' of when I first set eyes on you
Still thinkin' of all my better times

Many places I've never been, faces I don't know
I reckon I should've had a better a plan
These times, they sure are hard without you
But I'll still make the most of these old times

Life may never go as we plan
We can only keep lookin' ahead
I may never have much that's mine
But at least I still got some time
I promise that I'll be mighty fine
As long as I still got some time

Ron plucked the notes of the last two chords, ending the song in a small crescendo. He felt good playing and singing again. He wished that Betty could still hear him. He wanted to play another one, but his fingers were already getting too sore, so he gently sat the instrument back in its case.

"Mhm, mhm," he muttered to himself.

With nothing else left to do, Ron figured he should give Patsy a call.

NOTE FROM THE AUTHOR

The information regarding the history of Sol Legare and Mosquito Beach was pulled from these sources:

Samson, R. A Trip Back in Time: Mosquito Beach. *Discover South Carolina* https://discoversouthcarolina.com/articles/a-trip-back-in-time- mosquito-beach

Mosquito Beach History. *Historic Mosquito* https://www. historicmosquitobeach.com/home/history/

Pandolfi, E (2013) The Heart of Sol Legare. *Charleston City Paper* https://charlestoncitypaper.com/2013/02/06/the-heart-of-sol-legare/